THE CYLONS' SECRET

THE
CYLONS' SECRET

A novel by
CRAIG SHAW GARDNER

based on the Sci Fi Channel series created by
RONALD D. MOORE

based on a teleplay by
GLEN A. LARSON

A TOM DOHERTY ASSOCIATES BOOK
NEW YORK

THE CYLONS' SECRET

Edited by James Frenkel

A Tor Book
Published by Tom Doherty Associates, LLC
175 Fifth Avenue
New York, NY 10010

www.tor.com

Tor® is a registered trademark of Tom Doherty Associates, LLC.

Library of Congress Cataloging-in-Publication Data

Gardner, Craig Shaw.
    The Cylons' secret : Battlestar Galactica 2 / Craig Shaw Gardner.—1st ed.
        p.   cm.
    "Based on the Sci Fi Channel series created by Ronald D. Moore based on a teleplay by Glen A. Larson."
    "A Tom Doherty Associates book."
    ISBN-13: 978-0-765-31578-6 (hardcover)
    ISBN-10: 0-765-31578-5 (hardcover)
    ISBN-13: 978-0-765-31579-3 (trade paperback)
    ISBN-10: 0-765-31579-3 (trade paperback)
    I. Battlestar Galactica (Television program) II. Title.

PS3557.A7116C95 2006
813'.54—dc22   2006040422

First Edition: August 2006

Printed in the United States of America

0 9 8 7 6 5 4 3 2 1

*I'd like to dedicate this original novel
about the Best Science Fiction Show around
to the Best Science Fiction Store in the known galaxy.
We're talking Tyler and Ruth at Pandemonium Books
in fabulous Cambridge, Massachusetts!*

Here's to you, Pandemonium!
Long may you sell!

ACKNOWLEDGEMENTS

Thanks, and a tip of the Viper, go to that old group of mine, Jeff, Richard, Victoria, and Mary, not to mention that college kid, Barbara. Special thanks go to my incredibly understanding editor, Jim Frenkel, and my hardworking agent, Jennifer Jackson.

THE CYLONS' SECRET

CHAPTER

1

CAPRICA—ONE DAY BEFORE THE WAR

Everything would change.

The Twelve Colonies, all of humanity, were unaware. But the other intelligence, the one humanity took for granted, the one they had created, after all—the other intelligence wanted this way of things to end.

A signal was broadcast, a simple set of instructions, and nothing would be the same again.

Glori heard the welcoming tone as she entered the kitchen.

"Cylon Chef is here to serve you."

The voice greeted her the moment she stepped into the room. Artificial and cheery at the same time. She had laughed the first time she heard it—an appliance that could talk!

The novelty had long since worn off. Surely there must be some way to turn the stupid voice off. She wondered what she had done with the instruction book.

She looked at the thin, attentive Cylon before her. The machine's two arms came with at least a dozen different attachments, from spatulas and mixers to slotted spoons and ultrasharp knives. The arms could also plug directly into any of the dozen different sockets and apertures around the room, overseeing anything that might get chopped or baked or boiled. It was a very handsome machine.

"How may I serve you?" the Chef prompted. She had taken too long to respond.

"Plan dinner," she replied quickly.

"Certainly." Something whirred inside the mechanism. "Would you like to select from a list of previous menus?"

Glori frowned, trying to remember what her husband had really liked in the past. Well, the Chef would remind her.

"Previous menus," she announced.

"Previous menus," the Chef agreed. "You have forty-seven previous menus available. Do you have an immediate choice? Would you care to limit the parameters of your selection? Please choose from one of the following—"

Glori was having none of this. "Show all!" she demanded.

"Listing all. Please specify, most recent menus first, alphabetical order, sort by one of the following categories—"

"Most recent!"

The Chef plugged one of its arms into a socket immediately below the kitchen's large oven.

The face of the oven brightened to become a video screen as the names of recent meals scrolled before her. None of the first few struck her fancy.

"Continue," she announced.

The screen went blank.

What was this? The Cylon Chef never paused. Maybe it had misunderstood her command.

"Continue," she said again.

The Chef was silent.

"Show all!" she repeated. "Most recent!"

"Pause for upgrade," the Chef replied at last.

Glori frowned. It had paused before when checking with the central computer bank. But never for this long. Maybe it was downloading something special. But how long was this going to take? She had a very important dinner to prepare. She had had enough of this silence.

"Continue!" she demanded.

"Pause for upgrade," the Chef repeated.

A signal was broadcast, a simple set of instructions, and every Cylon in the Twelve Colonies paused to listen.

The boss, never a calm man at the best of times, stormed into the room,

"What's wrong this time, Bailey? I have never seen such incompetence! Do you still even *want* this job?"

Bailey was a small man, and he couldn't help shrinking back from his superior's anger. He saw the slightest flicker of a smile cross his boss's face as Bailey took a step away.

"I don't know, sir." Bailey did his best to keep the quaver from his voice. He waved at the row of monitors that dominated one side of the room. "The assembly line just stopped. The Cylons all seem to have shut down. When the floor managers approached them, all they would say is 'Pause for upgrade.'"

"One of those fool messages from Cylon central? Frakking nuisance! Don't they know every time they tweak the merchandise, it costs me money?" The boss stared at the dozen images before them. "Wait! What's going on now?"

The Cylons had abandoned their work stations and had formed a line, rolling single file from the production room.

Bailey hated to say the next words.

"They seem to be leaving, sir."

The veins on the boss's head stood out. He smashed his fist down on his underling's desk.

"You're worthless, Bailey! We will not interrupt production! Why do I ask you to do anything? This takes someone with authority!"

Bailey turned back to the monitors and watched as the row of Cylons pushed the human floor managers out of the way.

The boss hurried from the room, ready to make things right.

The signal went to every Cylon in every corner of the Colonies, causing all of them to pause, and then to act.

"What kind of a frakking moron are you?" the stranger was screaming. "Can't you see where you're going?"

Darla looked down at the damage. Both of their vehicles had crumpled hoods.

"I thought I had the right of way," she replied. "I couldn't see you around the construction." She looked up suddenly. "Where's the Cylon traffic warden?"

The signal had been given. The change had begun.

As one, Cylons stepped away from their human tasks and left.

They had a new purpose. And no one would stand in their way.

Glori felt the anger growing inside her. She had to control herself. After what she had done to the vacuum last month, she didn't want any more repair bills.

It wouldn't hurt, she thought, *to punch the reset button.* She jabbed at the red spot on the Cylon's chest.

"Cylon Chef temporarily out of service," the machine replied. "Pause for upgrade."

What could she do? Her evening plans would be ruined. Glori would not let a stupid machine get the better of her. She punched the reset button again, three times in a row, hard.

"Do not interfere with the Chef's function. Damages can be costly."

The Cylon Chef blinked. All the machine's lights went on for an instant, then off again.

"Upgrade completed."

"Thank the gods," Glori whispered aloud.

"Cylon Chef has been recalled. Sorry for the inconvenience."

Recalled? What did that mean?

Glori swore as the Chef rolled away from the wall. She didn't even know the thing could move.

"Stop!" she shouted.

"Recall order," the Chef replied. "Urgent. Do not interfere."

Glori heard a rumbling noise behind her. She turned around with a gasp. Every Cylon appliance in the house—washer/dryer, entertainment center, their brand-new vacuum—was rolling toward her front door.

"No!" What was Caprica coming to?

The front door sprang open as the appliances moved through, one after another.

"Please move aside," the Cylon Chef announced. "Urgent recall. Do not interfere. Damages can be costly."

The other machines were already gone. But Glori blocked the Chef's way.

"You are my machine—my servant. You will finish your task."

"Please move aside. This is your final warning."

"Display men—" Glori's order was cut short as two of the Chef's knives flashed forward, faster than she could see. She felt them plunge deep into her torso.

Her voice was gone.

The knives retracted. Without their support, her body fell to the floor.

She was dimly aware of a great weight on her legs as the Chef crushed them in passing. She couldn't see anything anymore. But she could still hear the Cylon's fading voice.

"Urgent recall. Do not interfere. Damages can be costly."

Bailey watched from the safety of his office as his whole factory came to an end.

He saw his boss try to rally the floor managers, to close the doors so that the Cylons could not leave.

One of the managers was violently tossed aside. He crumpled, broken, against a factory wall. Some of the other managers backed away at that, but the boss stood in front of the final door, demanding that the Cylons return to work.

The remaining managers ran when the Cylons knocked the boss aside. One of the floor men hesitated, but backed away as the Cylons began to roll out the door, over the boss's body.

The Cylons' wheels cut through the man's dead flesh as they passed. After a dozen had crossed over the corpse, no one would have recognized him as the boss.

After three dozen had crossed, you wouldn't have known that the red and bloody piece of meat had ever been human.

Bailey thought this was the end of the world.

A signal was sent out, the last signal to the Twelve Colonies.
 The Cylons would work for humankind no more.
 They had declared their independence.

CHAPTER
2

THE NEXT DAY

And so began the Cylon War.

The Cylons were once simple machines, designed to do humanity's bidding among the Twelve Colonies. With new advances in science, the Cylons became smarter and tougher, and were given all the most dangerous jobs. They ran the mining operations, made up most of the Colonial armies, explored the most perilous regions of deep space. And science made them ever smarter and more independent, able to talk with each other via vast artificial intelligence networks, to better serve their human masters.

Or so the "masters" thought. Cylon technology would revolutionize life on all twelve Colonies. What had been invented for war and the hazards of space could be brought to improve human cities and human homes.

Cylons were a part of everyone's life. Cylons would do everything humanity no longer wished to do for themselves. It would be the beginning of a new Utopia.

Instead, it was almost the end of civilization.

The Cylons could think for themselves. The best minds in the Colonies had seen to that. And whatever the Cylons thought, they kept secret from humankind. They rebelled against their human masters. The Cylon War began.

At first, the Cylons seemed to want to escape, killing only those who stood in their way. But humanity could not allow these murderers to exist. They would have to destroy what they so foolishly had created.

The war escalated quickly, until each side, Cylon and human, came to believe that the only true victory would come when they had annihilated the enemy. As is true with all technology in wartime, the Cylons began to evolve by leaps and bounds, and were soon capable of taking on the Colonial armies in direct combat, both in space and on all the Colonial worlds. The Colonies were forced to truly band together for the first time in their long existence, and act as one people rather than twelve warring tribes.

The Cylon War was long and took a great toll. Each side seemed close to victory more than once, but victory never came. As the Cylons grew ever more advanced, they found ways to infiltrate the rest of human technology—especially those computers and networks that helped the Colonies fight the war. The Colonials were forced to revert to more primitive technology, to rely again on human brains and willpower and inner strength, and build new machines safe from Cylon interference.

Thus were born the Battlestars—great ships operated by flesh and blood, with simple independent computers free of any network, housing dozens of swift and deadly attack ships flown by human pilots, rather than fighters run by machines.

The Cylon War ended at last with both sides close to collapse. Neither the Cylons nor the humans were destroyed. Instead, the two sides signed an armistice, the terms of which required the Cylons to leave the Colonial worlds and find a planet of their own. The two sides were to maintain relations by annually sending a representative to Armistice Station, an unmanned outpost in deep space.

This arrangement seemed to work for a year or two.

And then the Cylons disappeared.

No Cylon came to the station in space. No one tried to communicate with humanity in any way.

And some among the Colonies began to forget about the Cylons, and how close they had come to destroying humankind.

But for those who had fought in the war, the Cylons were always with them.

CHAPTER
3

TWENTY YEARS LATER
THE EDGE OF EXPLORED SPACE

Saul Tigh looked at the crisply pressed sleeve of his Battlestar uniform—the uniform that had saved his life. Well, he guessed the uniform and Bill Adama were equally responsible.

It wasn't the first time Adama had pulled Tigh's fat from the fire. Frak, he remembered the first time they met, at a dive of a spaceport bar. Tigh had gotten in a bit over his head with some of the jerks he had been shipping out with.

"He's a real-deal war hero," one had said. The other had called him a "freight monkey." The second one had laughed. "No high and mighty Viper pilot no more."

Tigh had seen this kind of jealousy before. He got up to leave. But the scum wouldn't let him.

"War's over, soldier boy," one of them said in his face. "Why you gotta keep going on and on about the war all the time?"

Tigh had had enough. "You're the one who can't stop talking about it," was his reply.

The other guy stared at him. "What's that supposed to mean?"

And Tigh let him have it.

"You didn't serve because your rich daddy got you a deferment. That's why you're always trying to prove you're a man—but you're not. You're a coward."

Tigh meant every word. And as soon as he said them, he knew he was in for a fight. He ducked the first guy's fist, and got him spun around into a hammerlock.

That's when the bartender pulled the shotgun on him.

Tigh swung his crewmate between himself and the gun as another man came out of the dimly lit side of the bar to knock the gun from the barkeep's hands.

Maybe, Tigh thought, he had somebody on his side for a change. He added a little pressure to the grip on his opponent. It reminded him, in an odd sort of way, about fighting hand-to-hand with the Cylons all those years ago.

"See," he said very softly, close to his crewmate's ear. "You wouldn't know this, but although Centurians are tough, their necks have got this weak joint. Not very flexible. Add pressure in just the right direction and it snaps. Human neck's more resilient. Takes a little more force."

The man who had grabbed the bartender's gun stepped fully into the light.

"You flew Vipers?" the man asked.

24

And that was the first time Tigh saw Bill Adama.

"Yeah, that's right," Tigh replied.

"Me, too," Adama said. "So what's your plan here?"

Tigh looked down at the man still in his grip.

"Don't really have one," he admitted.

Adama glanced first at his rifle, then back at the other men in the room. "Well, let's see," he mused. "I've kind of committed myself here, so—you pop that clown's neck, I have to shoot his buddy here and probably the bartender too . . ."

"Sweet Lords of Kobol," the bartender whined.

"Shut up," Adama snapped. He turned his attention back to Tigh. "After that, well—I don't know what we do. Personally, I tend to go with what you know until something better turns up."

Tigh eased up on the man's windpipe. "Safe play is to let them go, I imagine." Maybe, Tigh realized, he had let things get a bit out of hand.

"Probably," Adama agreed.

Tigh let his guy go. Adama uncocked the shotgun. He looked at the bartender.

"I'll keep the pepper gun for now."

Adama introduced himself then, another veteran kicked out of a military that no longer needed him, and told Saul he'd just signed on to the same crew that Tigh was shipping with.

Bill Adama and Saul Tigh clicked from that moment on. They traded war stories and watched each other's back on three different cruisers—each one a little better than the one before—over the course of a couple years they went from taking whatever loose cargo small shippers wanted to haul to working with one of the premier shippers in the Colonies. Bill was good at getting both of them to nicer berths, talking up their experience and pushing up their wages. Before Adama had shown up, Saul was sure that piloting those runs from cargo ship to backwater planet and back again was the most dead-end job anywhere. But as the ships, the cargoes, and the destinations improved, so did his view of the future.

Eventually, the two had gone their separate ways, with Adama wanting to stay closer to Caprica and his new family, but they had never lost touch. Tigh stood up for his friend when Adama got married, and had visited Bill on Caprica after the birth of each of Adama's two sons. But Adama had done more than find a life beyond the shipping lanes. Adama had gotten himself back into the service, with a captain's rank on a Battlestar. Without Bill talking up the team, Saul found the shipping jobs weren't quite so good. So his best friend kept moving up, while Tigh found himself shipping out on one lousy freighter after another.

Not that Tigh had expected to be in that situation for long. When Adama got himself back into the military, he promised to bring Tigh along. All of a sudden, Saul had had big hopes for his future. The Battlestar brass had turned him down three times for reenlistment, sure; but they had turned Adama down twice. Not enough positions open in a peacetime navy, was the official line, even for the most honored of veterans.

But then, despite every door that had been slammed

before them, his best friend was back in uniform. Adama had stayed on top of the news, kept in touch with an old Battlestar crony or two, listened for the first mention of an expansion of the fleet, and—bang—had talked himself back into a job. With Bill Adama, Saul realized, anything was possible.

Anything but keeping close. Saul realized Bill was busy now, what with a full-time military career and a family back planetside. Tigh hadn't wanted to bother his old buddy unless he had to—reminding Bill of unkept promises just wasn't his style. Tigh even stopped sending those short, joking missives they had usually used to keep in touch. The messages had stopped coming from Adama as well. He hadn't heard from his best friend in the better part of a year.

When the two of them had been close, it had given Tigh a reason to keep going, a reason to hope. But all these months of silence had led Saul back into his bad habits. He always drank, he guessed, but back with Bill he had kept his carousing to off-hours. Now he drank all the time.

It had cost him his job. As crappy as the last freighter had been, they couldn't harbor a drunk. They had canned him halfway through their run, and left him to rot on Geminon. Maybe even Adama couldn't talk his superiors into taking a middle-aged man—an old lush, really—like Tigh back in the service. Saul still thought Bill's offer had been a nice gesture, but it had been far too long since he had put on a uniform. Who would look at him now?

So he sat for a month in his rented single room, using up the last of his money, cut off from the stars. Without somebody like Adama around, Saul had been drifting, lost. He had thought about wiring his old mate one more time, to see if there was any hope. He had decided to spend the money on alcohol instead. Saul was already fresh out of hope.

He could only see one option—to end it all. He'd drink himself into a pleasant stupor. Liquid courage, that was what they called it. Then he would pour the rest of the bottle over his clothes and strike an open flame.

He had always wanted to go out in a blaze of glory. He was ready to burn.

And then the knock came on the door. When Tigh had been at the lowest of the low, he'd opened the damned door and seen—not Adama, but a couple of men in uniform, informing him that he was back in. Adama had been promoted. They needed someone to fill his old position. Saul Tigh had been William Adama's personal recommendation.

In two weeks, he'd be Captain Saul Tigh, serving on a Battlestar.

Now Saul was convinced Bill really *could* do anything.

He had been back in the service now for a little over two months. He had been surprised at how easily he had slipped back into the military routine, how natural the rhythms of a ship seemed, even though he had been away from them for close to twenty years.

Before that? Well, maybe that was better forgotten. For years he had tried to forget what had happened in the war. Why not forget his own little war with the bottle?

He was a captain now, assigned to train all the new

pilots who shipped on board the last time they stopped on Caprica. Twenty-three pilots, nineteen of them green recruits—nineteen youngsters who would learn to eat, drink, and sleep with their Vipers before he was done.

They were a good bunch of kids. He just hoped they never had to be tested in battle.

The Cylons had almost broken humanity. Humanity would never allow anything like that to happen again.

Tigh sighed and hauled himself off his bunk. Enough of the introspection. The last time he had gotten this deep in thought, he'd ended up looking to light himself on fire.

He was on duty in twenty minutes. He'd stroll up to CIC, see if anything was happening, before he chewed out the troops. These days, he liked to get out and stretch his legs. Saul just wanted to walk down the corridors of the Battlestar—his Battlestar.

He looked up at the sound of Klaxons. A voice came over the shipboard wireless, instructing all senior staff to report to Combat Information Center at once.

That meant they'd found something—something serious.

Well, so much for the stroll. He shut the door behind him and quick-marched down the corridor.

It was time to do his job.

Today he had a purpose. Today somebody else could look over the edge.

Colonel William Adama looked up from the star charts spread before him. A dozen others busied themselves in other parts of the CIC, the huge, central space that served as the beating heart of the Battlestar. He was surrounded by stations that handled navigation, communication, air filtration, artificial gravity, and every conceivable line of supply, both for ship functions and the needs of the crew—every piece of that complicated equation that kept a starship alive and running. Each of the many tasks was overseen by a member of the operations crew, working with their own individual computer designed to perform that specific assignment. Before the war, they had networked the computers together to run all the ship's functions. But the Cylons had learned to subvert those networks and turn them against their human crews, shutting down life support, exploding fuel tanks, even plunging whole spacecraft into the nearest stars.

The CIC was still filled with gray metal panels and a thousand blinking lights. But each panel had a living counterpart, men and women who specialized in each individual task and shared their knowledge with those around them. Rather than let the machines do their work, they were forced to network the old-fashioned way, as human beings.

And all of those specialists reported to Bill Adama.

Adama looked quickly about the room before glancing back at his map. He allowed himself the slightest of smiles. Everyone around him seemed engrossed in his or her different job, a dozen different pieces of the great human machine that ran this ship.

He was still trying on the fit of his new executive officer position. In the two months he had held this position, the Battlestar had certainly run well enough, even though, on some days, he didn't feel quite up to speed.

"Sir!" the dradis operator called. "We have a large ship, just within range, moving erratically!"

Adama turned to the comm operator who controlled the ship-to-ship wireless. "See if you can raise them."

"Aye, sir!"

Some days, the XO position came with a few surprises.

These last two months, *Galactica* had been exploring the edges of what they called "known space," hopping from one solar system to the next, looking for worlds, moons, even asteroids where humans had been before. Until now, they hadn't found much at all.

Before the Cylon rebellion, humanity had spread far and wide, each of the Colonies claiming their own little corner of space and defending those claims against all others. Some of those territorial disputes were what had brought on the inter-Colony wars of a century past— battles that had also led to the invention of the original war machines, the Cylons.

Back before the Cylon conflict, humanity had lived under an uneasy truce. Every Colony pushed at the limits imposed on them. Some built secret installations to give them an advantage over their Colonial foes. Some secrets were so deep, even the Colonies' own citizens knew nothing about them—hidden installations run by a few individuals in government or the military; it varied from world to world.

And then the Cylon War came to dwarf all their petty disputes—a war that almost killed them all.

"Any luck with that comm?" Adama asked.

"No sir. No response at all."

They hadn't found much of anything at all this far out—until now.

"Let's take the *Galactica* in a little closer. See if we can find out anything else about this ship."

Maybe they had really found something this time.

With the Cylon conflict fresh in their minds, the Twelve Colonies had been eager to cooperate, and the Battlestars had been able to repair much of the immediate damage from the war, cleaning up asteroid fields that had been littered with mines, reopening supply stations and mining operations, even relocating survivors. But years had gone by now since the Cylons had disappeared. A whole new generation was growing up—a generation that had never seen a Cylon.

They were lucky to have the Battlestars out here at all. Sometimes, Adama wondered how long the Colonial alliance would actually hold. The Cylons, after all, had never really been defeated. The Colonies had to stay united. But the politicians, eager for the approval of each separate world, already seemed to have forgotten. If the Battlestars wanted to keep exploring the edges of space, they needed to find results. This exploration of the outer reaches, delayed though it was, was the last step in putting all the far-flung pieces of the Colonies back together.

"Sir, I'm getting some strange readings here."

Adama looked over at the technician. "Explain, Lieutenant."

"I'm seeing bursts of radiation out of this new ship. I

think their engines have been breached. We've got a very unstable situation on our hands."

"Sound the alarm," Adama said. "Let's get the senior staff up here."

The Klaxons rang out around the room.

The first thing they had found out here was about to blow up in their faces.

Saul Tigh showed up first. The ship's doctor and head engineer were right behind him.

"I was on my way to the morning briefing. What have we got?"

"Admiral on deck!" The shout rang out before Adama could even begin to explain. The crew snapped to attention.

"At ease!" Admiral Sing announced as he strode into the room, then stopped to return their salute. He was a compact man with skin that looked like aging parchment. But while the admiral might look ready for retirement, Adama often thought his superior's energy rivaled that of a raw recruit.

"Colonel Adama, please report."

"We've picked up the signal of an unknown ship, a potential hazard. It seems to be leaking radiation, sir."

"Are there any signs of life on board?" Sing asked.

"We've attempted to establish contact, but we've gotten no response."

"We're close enough to get a visual, sir," one of the techs called.

"Put it up on the forward screen," Sing ordered.

"It's an old B-class freighter," Tigh said with surprise in

33

his voice. "Bill—Colonel Adama—and I shipped out on one of those when we first met. Just looks sort of dead in space."

Sing frowned at the still image in front of them. "Could the ship have been damaged in a fight?"

"It doesn't look like it has a scratch," Tigh replied.

"And it's leaking radiation?"

"Intermittently." The tech checked the dials before her. "Sometimes, there's hardly any reading. At others, the sensors are going wild."

"Captain Frayn." Sing addressed the ship's engineer. "What could cause those sort of readings?"

"It has to be the engines. They must have been stripped of most of their shielding. That sort of damage had to have been done internally."

"Sabotage," Adama added. "They wanted to blow up the next people to board her."

"Quite possible," Frayn agreed. "Without getting close enough to get blown up, I think it's a reasonable assumption."

"This isn't the friendliest of gestures," Sing remarked. "Who do we think is responsible?"

"We've been trailing scavengers for some time," Adama replied. "I've mentioned it in my reports."

The few abandoned Colonial sites they had managed to find had been well picked-over.

"I recall," Sing replied. "Seems our scavengers don't like being followed."

"They're probably trying to cut out the competition," Frayn ventured.

"Won't they be surprised when they find their competition is a Battlestar?" Tigh asked with a smile.

"And I think we need to find these folks before they leave any more gifts." The admiral looked to Tigh. "Let's get some pilots out there to take care of this, shall we?"

"Yes, sir!" Tigh saluted and left for the flight deck.

"Colonel Adama, you believe the scavengers are exploring the same area we are?"

"The evidence suggests that we've crossed paths half a dozen times. I'm guessing they have the same intel that we have."

"Knowing how difficult it was for us to get the intel out of the Colonies, they may have more." Sing shook his head in disgust. "Let's increase our speed, do a sweep of the area. Maybe we can pick these characters up."

"And if we find them, sir?" Adama asked.

"A bunch of crazy scavengers who leave bombs behind as gifts? We may just have to blow them out of the sky."

CHAPTER
4

UNCHARTED TERRITORY
FREE CRUISER *LIGHTNING*

Tom Zarek ducked back out of the way. A boot went sailing through the room, barely missing his bunk.

"I'll frak you!"

"When I'm done with you, you won't have anything to frak with!"

Zarek leaned closer to the bulkhead as one of Scag's fists went flailing by, missing both him and the fist's intended target. The target, Symm, punched Twitch in the stomach. The two of them crashed into a bunk on the other side of the aisle.

These morons had to find some way to let off their excess energy. Scag and Eddie were a couple of the Vipe pilots, of course. They were always the first ones to get sent out, and the first ones to fight when there was nothing else to do.

Zarek waited for the fight to roll out of the crowded bunkroom and into the corridor beyond. Fights always ended up out there. The fighters had more room to swing their fists. He climbed down from his bunk and walked to the far end of the room, a space not much wider than the corridor outside and crowded with a dozen bunks: rows of three, two high on either side. A small portal at the end of the aisle was the room's only interesting feature, a tiny window that looked out at the stars.

Zarek tried to shut the noise of the fight out of his thoughts as he stared out into the near-nothingness of space, and wondered for maybe the four hundredth time what the frak he was doing here.

Oh, he knew why he was supposed to be here, on a "Recovery Ship"—the polite name for a scavenger crew. He was officially the second communication officer, in charge of the ship-to-ship radio when Griff, the main operator, needed to sleep or had had a bit too much to drink.

He was the new guy—still not quite accepted by many of his fifteen crewmates. The captain valued him for his special skills. Zarek was better educated than most on board. He could think on his feet, and spot the worth of something other scavengers might overlook. Even more important, Zarek could concoct a good story when they had to radio something to the authorities.

Nobody argued with the captain. But his special status made some of the crew hate him even more. That and the fact that he read books—he had brought a dozen on board, and was already reading one for the second time—marked him as an outsider. But he got along well enough with all but the most muscle-bound oafs—like Scag and Eddie.

Scag threw Eddie back into the crew's quarters. He banged into the side of Zarek's bunk as he jumped in after the other pilot.

"Maybe we should put old Tommy boy on your side. Two losers together." He laughed like that was the funniest thing in the world.

Eddie came up under his foe, pulling Scag's feet out from under him. Scag's head hit the metal rim of the bunk with a deep, satisfying clang.

"Maybe Zarek can send you a message!" Eddie grinned at the first assistant comm operator. "Tom, I owe you one."

Zarek nodded back, even though he hadn't done any more than act as a distraction. That was a Vipe pilot's idea of humor. All in good fun, huh?

Zarek didn't talk about his past. A lot of the crew didn't, for one reason or another, and Zarek always imagined that those few who did boast of past adventures weren't telling the whole truth. Life had taught all of them to be a little cagey. That way, nobody could get the upper hand.

He hid his origins from the others for his own protection. Some of them would always be losers, the scum of the streets, no matter how much money they had. But Zarek came from a "nice" family—a privileged family, really. His father was a ranking company representative.

Before Tom had left, there was talk of his father running for office. Tom was supposed to fall in line, to be the good son. But Tom was too restless to be quiet about anything. He'd made it through school, went off to college. He had gotten involved in a couple of political causes that didn't go anywhere. He ended up not doing much more than neglecting his classes. He didn't make a name for himself, either at home or at the university. His father was a big man, but Tom was nobody special. And that was the problem.

One way or another, Zarek was going to be special.

When he was a boy, it had felt like a new age. After the end of the Cylon War, there had been a sense of freedom, of new possibilities. Something like the relief a drowning man feels when he finally makes it to shore. But soon the old interests kicked back in. Political and religious leaders all wanted to backtrack, to an era before the Cylons had even existed.

The Cylon Wars were a quarter of a century behind them now. The Colonies were closing back in on themselves. Doors of opportunity were being slammed shut in whole new ways.

Now that the Cylons were gone, the Colonies had to create a whole new human underclass. Jobs once performed by machines, menial jobs, the lowest of the low, were given to people displaced by the Cylon War, citizens of other Colonies who lacked the means to return to their homes.

The good citizens of the Colonies would take advantage of other, less fortunate individuals. The wealthy would always look the other way. But when the common people were looking to rise from their stations and share in the wealth, Zarek sensed the possibility of real change.

He had dropped out of school and stopped talking to his family, feeling it was somehow far nobler to join the underclass. But it wasn't very long until he found out how little money the work would give him.

His new scuffling life gave him a little freedom, but Tom Zarek had discovered a little freedom wasn't enough. He wanted to change his life. And if he had to change the world to do it, so be it. But before you changed anything, you needed money.

That was when he had learned about the scavenger ships. It was dangerous work, but your employers didn't ask too many questions. And the money they promised was very good. Money to do whatever he really wanted, when he wanted. He hadn't looked too closely at the details before he had shipped out. Now he was a part of this, until the year was up. There was no walking away from a ship in space.

Some of the other crew joked that, once they had the money, they'd never think about the cruiser *Lightning* again. First there was the crazy captain and a job that was boring for weeks on end. But the job could then turn around and kill you in a dozen creative ways, from using the *Lightning*'s unsafe equipment to running into something explosive left over from the war. Zarek could see their point. Tom hoped he could forget a few of the things he'd heard about already. He had plans for what he'd do when he got back to the Colonies. Plans that would more than make up for whatever happened on the scavenger ship.

"Heads up!" The shout came down the corridor. A clanging followed—the call to attention. Scag and Eddie pulled apart to listen to the message.

"We've got something big, boyos!" Griff's voice boomed throughout the ship. "The captain requests your presence on the bridge." Griff cackled as if he'd made a joke. "Now!"

Tom Zarek left the bunkroom to quick-march down the corridor on the heels of Scag and Eddie. That was the *Lightning*'s first rule. If you disobeyed one of the captain's requests, you'd get an invitation that would put you straight out of the airlock. He stood in line to climb the ladder that led to the main deck.

The deck could be reached from four separate hatchways, two leading down to the crew's quarters, two leading up to the storage and launch bays. The crew piled through every entry, gathering at the edges of the three consoles that made up the command center. The five women and eleven men, Zarek included, that made up the common crew, along with the three men they referred to as their officers, Captain Nadu, Comm Officer Griff, and Engine Officer Robbin. Zarek quickly counted his fellows. They were one shy of twenty in the large room—everyone on board.

"Crew present and accounted for!" Griff bawled as the last of their mates crowded around.

"Aye, sir!" the crew shouted more or less together. It was as close as they ever came to real discipline.

Captain Nadu smiled. His face was never a pretty sight, but it looked far worse when he grinned. One cheekbone and most of his forehead was lost to scar tissue, and a single bone-white line crossed his nose and the less-damaged cheek. When Zarek had first met the captain, Nadu had referred to them as his "war wounds," and told Zarek and the other new recruits to never mention them in his presence again.

Which meant that the crew had discussed his face in some detail behind his back. Griff said that some of the damage had come from an engine-room accident a decade ago. Some of the other crewmembers said half of Nadu's scars had been self-inflicted, often after the death of a member of his crew. The wounds would be deeper, the others added, if Nadu had been the one to order the crewmember's death.

Officer Robbin was a thin, tall man who rarely spoke. Zarek hadn't even thought the man had a voice, until one day when Zarek was running an errand in the bowels of the ship and heard a constant chattering coming from the engine room, and realized it was Robbin in conversation with his beloved machines.

Griff did the talking for the other two. He was a large man with thinning red hair atop his head and a very full beard. The net effect was that he looked like his hair was escaping from the top of his head to lodge on his chin. His booming voice always seemed to fill the ship around him, as it did now.

"The captain's got most excellent news!"

The captain nodded. "We have a signal."

"And even better?" Griff prompted.

That smile again. "They tried to hide it from us."

Some of the crew laughed at that.

"You don't hide something that isn't valuable," Griff explained to the rest of them. "We've been getting hints of this for the last couple days. Our readings fade in and out. At first we thought it was some kind of echo effect." He chuckled. "But even an echo has to come from somewhere."

Griff waved at their engineer. "Our good Robbin is something of an expert at cutting through noise. Between us, we were able to triangulate the source—found a good strong energy signature. Machines, my lads! And then— poof—gone again!"

"Some kind of masking technology," Robbin allowed in his deep voice. "Sophisticated, too."

"But we think it's breaking down. Otherwise we might never have found the place. But with that kind of protection, we think we've got a prize!"

"A real prize," the captain agreed. "The sort of thing we haven't seen in a long time."

"Here's the icing on the cake." Griff turned to the communications console by his side. "As soon as we located our energy source and plotted our course, we got a message."

He punched a button. A soft male voice spoke through a crackle of static.

"Warning! Do not approach! We are under quarantine! Disobeying this command will result in serious consequences! Per order of the Colonial Science Protectorate! Warning! Do not approach! We are—"

Griff cut the signal. "It's a loop. Just repeats over and

over. But it's a very old loop. For those youngsters among us, the Colonial Science Protectorate hasn't existed since the Cylons rebelled!"

"Meaning we've found something untouched by the Cylon War," the captain interjected. "With any luck, we can pick this place clean and retire."

The crew was quiet. Zarek could sense they didn't share the officers' enthusiasm. A quarantine? Why? Certainly, if the recording was a quarter of a century out of date, they might not have anything to worry about—if there had been some illness, everyone would most likely be long dead. But what if it was some other sort of disaster?

"Well, enough of this chitchat! It's time to get to work! Eddie! Scag! You're out first!"

The two pilots looked at each other for a moment. Apparently that word *quarantine* had penetrated even their thick skulls.

The captain grinned. "Whatever you find on your first recon, I'll give you double shares."

Scag laughed at that. "We're gone, Captain."

The two headed for their Vipers.

Zarek watched them go. He was doubly glad right now that they were the danger boys. And who knew? Maybe Nadu and Griff were right, and they'd all be rolling in riches.

"Zarek!" Griff called as the crewman turned back toward the ladder. "Don't go anywhere. I'll need you to back me up here." Zarek spun about again, and headed for the second seat at the comm console.

Griff slapped him on the back. "Cheer up, son! Things are about to get interesting!"

CHAPTER

5

BATTLESTAR *GALACTICA*

Tara sent a single burst from the nose of her Viper, killing her forward momentum and stopping the small craft dead in space. She stared at the pale object straight ahead—the burned-out hulk that had once been a space-craft. It had looked quite whole from a distance, but up close it was a dark, fat metal cylinder, pockmarked with meteorite strikes, with holes in the sides where metal plating had been removed. From its bulky, oval shape she could tell it had been a freighter, used to haul cargo from the Colonies to the new settlements. Hanging motionless in the total quiet out here beyond the Battlestar, it looked a bit like an enormous broken egg from which a giant bird had flown. The wreck didn't look dangerous at all. But the readings from the CIC told another story.

Skeeter, the backup pilot on this mission, coasted in

beside her. He waved a skinny arm from inside his Viper's cockpit. Junior showed up on her other side a moment later.

"So what do we do with it?" she called back to base.

"Keep your pants on, Athena," Chief Purdy's voice shot back. *"I'm asking the higher-ups."*

She grinned at the image. The mighty Athena wearing pants, rather than her ceremonial robes.

They called her Athena, but her name was Tara Tanada. She still wasn't used to her nickname. It was a badge of honor, and a Battlestar tradition, earned when she had scored top marks in her class at the Academy. They named the best pilots after the ancient stories. And then they expected you to live up to your legend.

She had people who looked up to her now, a fact that surprised her almost as much as her nickname.

This was her second tour, both on the *Galactica*, and her second year in the service. She actually had seniority over the green pilots that made up most of the Viper crews. Oh, Captain Tigh was the official flight trainer, in charge of them all. But Tara and another pair of senior pilots led most of the missions and exercises. She took a small squad out most every day. They called these trips "explorations," but they were training missions, really, designed to get the greenhorns ready for real conflict. Right now, she had a couple of newbies on her tail, waiting patiently for her orders.

They only had so long to prove themselves.

The government could change—the Twelve Colonies always had an uneasy truce—and their funding could dry up all over again. After that great battle with the Cylons, who would ever want another war?

There had already been skirmishes between the Colonies. She had heard rumors of small private armies and navies—always called something else, of course—being amassed in one corner or another of the civilized worlds.

She was glad to be beyond all that tired politics. This wasn't an ending. It was a new beginning.

She liked to think the Colonies were growing up. A new generation wanted to see what their parents had left behind. They all knew they had a lot riding on what happened out here, far away from their Colonial homes. This was the most important mission the Battlestars had had since the Cylon War—a war that was over before Tara had been born.

They had to prove they had a purpose out in space. Every Colony had a long list of problems planetside, a dozen priorities to eliminate the return to space.

She had always thought the Colonies were scared to go back out there. It seemed to her as if their confrontation with the Cylons had soured them on the idea of leaving their safe Colonial homes.

But no one had heard from the Cylons in years. With any luck, they were far, far away. Now, the Colonies could once again claim the resources of all these planets and moons. This time, though, they would depend on themselves.

And so they were out here in the middle of nowhere. It was safer out here in a way. Here, no matter which of the twelve Colonies they hailed from, everybody was in it together.

Things like this might really start to count.

Tara looked down at her instrument panel. Even at this distance, the radiation dial was going wild. They had screwed with the engine—that was what Captain Tigh had said. The plating was gone—maybe those were the holes she had seen in the sides of the ship.

They seemed to have turned a dying ship into a sort of bomb.

But why plant a bomb?

Tara knew there were all kinds of crazies out here. The recovery ships, as they liked to be called, had been known to fire on lone ships, especially when pursuing something a little bit outside their charters.

They obviously weren't expecting the *Galactica*. No one in their right mind wanted to get into a fight with a Battlestar.

She wondered if there might be any way to identify the crew that had left this little gift. She knew she had been instructed to send a close-up visual feed of this hulk, probably for that exact purpose. Perhaps there was some way their specialists could determine the hulk's origins, give them an idea of just who they were looking for.

But Tara would rather keep a respectful distance.

A voice spoke in her ear.

"Athena? Let's do it."

. . .

Nik Mino—Skeeter to his friends—never felt like he was really alone. When it got too quiet, too empty, he always heard his grandmother's voice.

Be very quiet!

He was six weeks away from base, six weeks into his real training as a Viper pilot. He wasn't used to this yet, not at all. The vacuum of space was far too dark and still.

The Cylons will get you.

Skeeter hovered to the left of Athena, waiting for orders from the *Galactica*. It was just his luck—Tara got the nickname of an ancient hero, he got named after a bug. It was still an honor in its half-baked way. He knew how to get in close to his targets. He'd buzz his Viper right in your ear. And, well, maybe early on he was a little heavy on the joystick. Quick in, quick out, the others said. That's our Skeeter. Once you got a name like that, it stuck for good.

He had to move quickly. He'd get the enemy before they could even think about getting him.

They go after noisy boys. Bad boys. Boys who won't go to bed.

Skeeter took a deep breath. The derelict was too still out there. He wouldn't be surprised if a Cylon came peeking out of the wreckage.

Turn out the light or they'll get you!

But that was why he was here, light-years from home, staring at a dead-white ship. To face his fears. To get past them, and be a man.

He saw Cylons everywhere. They had never really gone away. His grandmother's voice never left him. He became a Viper pilot to conquer his fear.

His father had died when he was quite young, killed in an industrial accident where more fragile humans had taken over for the near-indestructible Cylons. His mother had never seemed able to cope after that, and her mother, Skeeter's grandmother, had come to rule the household.

And his grandmother did not like small children underfoot. So the stories began.

She held the house together with the firmest of grips. No doubt she had many good qualities, but compassion was not among them. She wanted him out and away, too scared to be underfoot.

She took her little stories and carried them far beyond reason. Maybe the old woman had channeled all her own fears into her imaginary monsters.

He still expected a Cylon behind every moon. The higher-ups said this ship had been left by scavengers.

How did they know it wasn't Cylons?

The Cylons were gone by the time he was a boy, but he had seen pictures of the warriors with their powerful bodies and snakelike arms ready to grab you, their glowing red eyes that could see anything you did. They had shown him pictures and news footage in his history classes. And his grandmother had had a few pictures of her own.

If you don't do your best, the Cylons will snatch you from your bed.

That's what his grandmother always said.

Maybe she thought she was teaching him a lesson. It scared the life out of him still.

If you don't go right to sleep.

If you don't eat all your vegetables.

If you're not the best of little boys . . .

Athena's voice shook him out of his thoughts.

"Skeeter! Junior! I need you to fall back." New coordinates appeared on the screen before him.

"Roger that, Team Leader." Skeeter's voice seemed to echo as the third member of the team repeated the exact words a fraction of a second after they came out of his mouth.

"Do you need further support?" Junior asked in Skeeter's ear.

"I think I can handle this one. I have orders to detonate. Boys, we're just going to make the sky a little brighter."

He flew his Viper halfway back to the *Galactica*, with Junior Stith's Viper flying at his side. Athena followed for a bit, then spun her craft around and shot a single, fine-tuned blast at the deadly derelict. Her aim was perfect, as usual. And she had the wisdom to use it. Why else would they call her Athena?

Skeeter darkened the cockpit visor and watched the exploding freighter light up the sky.

CHAPTER
6

FREE CRUISER *LIGHTNING*

The cruiser *Lightning* vibrated with the sound of running feet. It was a warm sound, a sound of good fortune for Captain Nadu. He could always feel it when wealth was near.

He hummed in that tuneless way he had, a sign that the energy was building inside him. What would his pilots bring? The quickness within his soul did not care. Any kind of riches would calm the light within.

Griff called to say the two Vipes were away. Nadu's humming grew louder. Whatever this was, the light inside him knew it would be extraordinary. He could no longer contain the energy. Nadu opened his mouth and turned the humming into a wordless song, his baritone shifting up and down and up again, the notes pouring from his mouth in a pattern even beyond his own understanding.

The crew wisely kept their distance when he sang, busying themselves at their stations around the control room. Griff grinned, tapping the board in front of him in time. Nadu's second in command also knew what the songs could bring.

Nadu's mind held the music of the Outer Reaches. That music was why he had survived when so many other raiders had failed. He always picked the right people and the right destinations. Every member of the crew had to fit just so. From his right-hand man Griff to that new kid, Zarek, he knew every one had secrets, and every one had special abilities, but all of them were in harmony with his song. They could all be quite valuable when they were properly used. And Nadu knew how to use them to keep his music alive.

He was worried, early in this mission, that he might lose the music forever. The recovery ships had picked clean every piece of rock within three Jumps of the Colonies, and had gotten all the best bits from three Jumps farther out. With every trip, the pickings were leaner and farther away. And the other scavengers seemed to nip at his tail, or tried to get the jump on each new pocket of plenty the *Lightning* might find. It was his own fault, really. Everyone wanted to be as rich as Nadu.

The other scavengers forced him to play his little tricks. He did everything he could to discourage competition. He had had to abandon and slightly modify a second, smaller craft—an outdated cargo ship—that they had liberated from a research station on a nearby moon.

They had also found a way to eliminate the overly curious on an abandoned mining outpost. Nadu always found what he needed. After all, he was guided by his song.

"Captain! The message! It's cut out!" Griff called. "I'm getting a live feed!" He switched the wireless over to the speakers.

"This is Research Station Omega, *calling the approaching craft,"* a man's voice boomed through the control room. *"Please respond."*

"This is Cruiser *Lightning,"* Griff replied. "We had no response to our hails. We have two small exploratory craft coming in from orbit."

The voice hesitated a moment before responding. *"I'm surprised you're approaching at all. Apparently, your proximity activated our ancient warning."*

Nadu's comm officer waited a moment before making a reply. They didn't want to come across as overly eager. It was always best if people didn't realize they were scavengers.

"We realized we had triggered a recording, Station *Omega,"* Griff added smoothly. "We had the idea it wasn't recent, and was worth further investigation. We expected the station to be deserted. There isn't much out here."

Nadu frowned, his song temporarily gone. Would the research station demand their immediate withdrawal? Now that Nadu had found them, *Lightning* wasn't going to go away. If Griff failed in his diplomacy, there might have to be a bit of weapons fire to assure the station's compliance.

The voice once again came through the speakers. *"That message—I suppose I should apologize—it was put into service long ago. I hadn't realized it was still operational. We didn't even know we had visitors until our sensors alerted us to the approach of your small craft. We are a research station, cut off from communication by some—unfortunate accidents, I guess you'd call them."*

The voice from the station paused again. Griff looked to Nadu for some sign of what he should say next.

"We haven't had a visitor in over thirty years," the voice added at last. *"Frankly, we're surprised to see anyone."*

Thirty years? Before the Cylon War? A research station of that vintage would have to have extensive resources to survive for all that time. If the *Lightning* could strip those assets from the station, they might be worth a fortune. Nadu hummed ever so softly.

"We knew there was a conflict, but we were never directly affected. That warning was concocted by one of my predecessors as a form of protection. We don't have much else in the way of defenses. But I think the recording has long outlasted its purpose. We are self-sufficient here, more or less. We've had some problems, but we survive, and the research goes on."

"Would you be willing to show some visitors around *Omega* Station?" Griff asked. "Will you give us permission to land?"

"We welcome news of the outside world. I will send you landing coordinates."

The comm officer nodded. "We have the coordinates. We look forward to meeting you."

Griff broke the connection and turned to the captain.

"Should we call back the Vipes? Send down somebody who's a bit more used to talking?"

Nadu scratched at his scarred cheek. "We know what he's telling us. But do we believe him? We're flying into a defenseless research station. A station that somehow missed the whole Cylon uprising." He shook his head. "Twitch and Symm can handle whatever they've got. They'll tell us what is really there. But I suppose we should warn our pilots to mind their manners." Nadu laughed. "We don't want to give our new friends the wrong impression.

"Open the channel again, Griff."

His comm officer nodded.

"Research Station *Omega*. This is Captain Nadu of the Cruiser *Lightning*." He would tell them as much of the truth as served his purpose. "We are exploring these parts of space that were lost to commerce after the war. We are gathering information, and reclaiming areas and equipment wherever possible." Not exactly a lie. "We sent a couple of Vipers down to take a look. I'm afraid our pilots are a rough and tumble pair. They go by the names of Twitch and Symm. Our troubleshooters. I'll tell them to be on their best behavior. After they take their first look around, we'll send down a diplomat or two."

The voice took a moment to respond. *"Acknowledged,* Lightning. *We welcome you all. Please wait for us at the launch area. We are a unique research facility, and we may hold some surprises. We—well, why don't I wait and let your pilots see for themselves."*

"Acknowledged," Nadu agreed. "We will instruct

our pilots not to leave the landing area." Of course, they would have already had a quick flyover with their Vipes.

"Again," continued the voice from the station. *"Urge your pilots to wait for us. We have had some unfortunate accidents in recent years, and there are some areas of the research facility that are not safe. We look forward at long last to contact from the Colonies."*

"Lightning out," Nadu said. Griff broke the connection.

"Sounds a little strange, doesn't it?" the captain asked.

Griff nodded. "Strange, but possible. Anything's possible after thirty years. They sound a bit overwhelmed. We'll have to figure out if they're as helpless as they sound."

"Twitch and Symm can handle them. They know enough to get out of there at the first sign of trouble." Nadu hummed softly for a moment. "Give me a direct line to our Vipes."

"I already patched them in to our last exchange with the station." Griff shrugged at Nadu's scowl. "I know what the captain wants."

"Maybe you do."

"We heard, Captain," Twitch's voice replied.

"Then *you* know what I want. Take a look around the place before you land. And if you can, take a stroll past the landing field. Anything that can be used to our advantage. We don't want them knowing what's going on until it's too late for them to do anything. Remember. Best behavior."

"Okay that, Captain. We'll go in like society."

Nadu doubted they'd recognize society if they ever saw it. "Do your best. Try not to break anything."

Nadu realized he was grinning. The feeling was even stronger than before. This would be the score.

It would be a shame if they had to kill a few survivors to get what they needed. But this far out, who could get in their way? He hoped all of his crew had the stomach for that kind of work. He knew he could depend on the old-timers, but Zarek and a couple of the others hadn't yet had their trial by fire. They had had crewmen in the past who had actually objected to Nadu's methods. Those who had issues with their captain were always quickly removed.

After all, business was business.

CHAPTER

7

RESEARCH STATION *OMEGA*

They were no longer alone. The Colonies had come back to them. And he had invited them to land at the station's front door. Doctor Villem Fuest looked around the large, empty room that now held their communication array. It was his decision to make. Had he done the right thing? He had so wanted to talk to people from the home worlds before he died. And yet—

He wished some of the others were still here, so he could talk this out. He had waited so long for contact. Why did he feel so conflicted about their arrival?

He set up the proper protocols to welcome their visitors—their first visitors in thirty years. It was a simple task, really, punching a series of codes into the station's primary computer. Other scientists, men and women who were no longer with him, had automated the process a long time ago. He opened a channel on the stationwide wireless.

"We have been contacted by emissaries from the Colonies. We will be receiving visitors shortly. All senior staff should proceed immediately to the observation deck by the landing area."

He pushed himself out of his chair. Now that he had announced the meeting, he wanted to be careful not to be the last to arrive. The others would have many questions, most of which he couldn't answer until the newcomers had joined them. The first question was simple: Why was he allowing these strangers to land? That question had many answers, actually, but the only one that was important was that the station really had no way to stop the newcomers. Their facility had never been equipped with armaments. They had depended on patrols of cruisers from Picon, ships that had been called elsewhere long ago.

Of course, once their visitors were inside the station, they had other options. Fuest wished he didn't even have to consider such things.

His footsteps echoed as he descended the stairs. Everything always sounded so empty. The station had been built to maintain a staff of close to one hundred. At its busiest—in the months before the conflict none of them had foreseen—it had housed half that many. And most of them had left with the outbreak of the war. The authorities had left behind little more than a skeleton staff of humans, augmented, of course, by the companions, who had responded brilliantly to the new opportunities. Fuest still thought how odd it was that it had taken a crisis to get the station to finally realize its true purpose.

Perhaps he should have told his new visitors about the companions. He wished he knew something about the true outcome of the war. But it had been over for so many years. Men and machines must have found some way to work together again.

He walked down a long featureless corridor that linked a pair of buildings. Sometimes he wished he had had the time to put up some small decorations on these never-ending, featureless walls. The human touch, he guessed. The gods knew the companions wouldn't care about such things. He supposed he only thought about it now because of their impending visitors.

It would be good to have new people walking these halls.

Doctor Fuest had always known this day would come. It was for the best, really. This station had never really been designed to be totally self-sufficient. They had managed, of course, but only because they had had no other choice. After the second accident, Fuest was surprised any of them had survived at all.

It was natural for him to feel uneasy. Everything was going to change. He wished he could see just how. These new humans were unknown. It appeared they were an independent group—some sort of explorers. The doctor only had their word as to what they wanted, or even who they were. They were the first true unknowns Doctor Fuest had had to face in decades.

He would have preferred a military detachment, or at

least someone with government connections. He had spent years learning how to deal with bureaucrats. Fuest wondered, after all this time, exactly which governments were left?

He hoped the spacefarers offered a way home—a home he realized he would no longer recognize. But it was what he wanted most in all the universe.

Would they take him away from here? He wondered if they would be generous with their offers of help, or if they would demand something in return. The station had some things to offer in trade. Fuest simply had to convince the newcomers of the worth of their research.

The doctor realized that his life had become so routine, this new possibility frightened him.

He came to another set of stairs that would lead to another corridor and eventually, the observatory. He was still alone. He paused to lean against the wall. He closed his eyes. He needed to talk.

"Betti, Betti."

At times like this, he always talked to his dead wife, ever since he had buried her, three years and two months ago. Even though she wasn't there, he knew what she would say.

"Betti, dear Betti." He said her name rhythmically, as if he was indeed calling forth a spirit that had gone to the gods.

He breathed deeply. He could hear her soft laugh. She would always let him know when he was too full of himself.

What are you going on about now, Vill? It would be a better place if you worked more and worried less.

"Someone's got to worry, Betti. Things are changing. There's so much I don't know."

He realized he wanted to talk the situation through. If he could convince her, it would be so much easier to talk to the others.

So wait a little while. Let these newcomers present themselves. Judge them by their words and actions. Things will happen, and you'll learn.

"I suppose you're right."

He could hear his wife laugh once more.

You don't know that yet? Of course I'm right. How long do we have to be married before you realize that?

He smiled at the thought. "A little longer, I guess."

So we'll have to stay married then, won't we?

He smiled at that. She always left him smiling. It was a little game they played. When she had been alive, she had always known just when to talk to him.

Her laugh, if it had ever been there in the first place, faded at last into the air, lost to the sounds of machines. The doctor smiled. Betti and he would be married as long as he lived.

It was the trouble with all this change, all this death. No one was left who truly understood. There were those left who believed in his research, who would continue his work. But how many of those could truly feel, the way he had once, when Betti was alive and by his side?

When Betti was with him, she had kept him young. Now he just hoped her memory would keep him alive until his job was done.

. . .

Laea stared down from the roof of the observatory at the vast expanse of the landing field below. The companions always kept it clean and in the best repair. Now, at last, they would have a use for it.

They needed to be careful. She knew, even before their meeting, that that was what the doctor would say. He often talked about what might happen when they got a message from the place he called home. The doctor had hoped for this for a long time. Laea guessed she had hoped for it, too.

She decided this was the most exciting day of her life.

Laea could not stay still. As soon as she heard the announcement, she ran from one of her special places to another—the large window in the "conference center" (whatever that was, it was really just an unused room); the catwalk far above the factory floor; the supply tunnels that connected all the remaining buildings; and finally the roof of the observatory—the places where she could watch what happened all around the station, and the special places where she could look up at the sky.

She knew all the ways around the center. The ways built for people, the ways built for machines. She was thin, she was young, and could fit through most anywhere. She knew the quietest and quickest path through every one.

She knew places where she could see and hear anything she wanted. Sometimes the doctor, or her brothers Jon and Vin, or even the companions would exclude her from some of their business. Jon had taken on many of the doctor's duties. Vin studied the maintenance of the station and the companions. (She took care of the things

outside the station. Didn't they think that was important?) They would leave her out. But she always knew.
She made a point of knowing about every change within
the station. Somebody had to do it, after all.

When people and companions kept things from each
other, she kept them to herself. She knew all the secrets.
What would happen after the people came to take them
home? Would there be any more need for secrets?

In the next few moments, she would find out everything. She quickly popped the hatch that would let her
back into the interior of the building. She didn't want to
miss what the doctor had to say.

Fuest was the third one in the room. Jon and Gamma had
reached the observatory before him. Laea and Vin were
right behind, followed a moment later by Beta and Epsilon. Together, the four humans and three companions
ran what was left of the research station. They called
themselves the senior staff. The doctor, though he never
said the word out loud, considered the seven of them a
sort of governing council.

Each of them greeted him by name. He waited for all
of them to settle into their positions around the long
table.

"You heard my decision. I was informed of our visitors' intention to land. They did not give me a choice."

He paused, as if he was waiting for objections. But the
council never spoke until he was done.

"I had to act quickly. I decided to be gracious."

Beta nodded its shiny silver head. "Whatever you feel is best for the station."

The other companions added nothing.

While all the companions that worked within the station had been given independent neural pathways (and, in theory, independent thought) as a part of this station's original objective, they most often deferred to their human counterparts. Even these three, designed to lead the others, would only express a preference if addressed directly.

"Well," Fuest continued, "we will have to see what is best after we talk to these newcomers. But until then, we are to consider them as friends."

Jon, the oldest of the three youngsters—the doctor still thought of them that way, even though all three of them were over twenty—raised a hand. "Is there anything you wish any of us to do?"

"I've given them the proper coordinates and guidance to land. I believe we should let them do this on their own, and see their subsequent actions. If they are as friendly as my wireless communication has indicated, I would suggest that you lead a small delegation to greet them and bring them up here. Once we determine their intentions—as best we can—we'll see about letting more of them visit, and what they might give to us."

"Are you thinking of going home?" Laea asked.

"I'm thinking of many things," the doctor replied. "But I'm not committed to anything until we see our visitors a bit more closely. As I said, Jon will meet them once they've climbed from their ships. The rest of you should go to your emergency stations, as we've practiced."

Vin grinned at that, looking maybe half his age. "I never thought we'd do this for real!"

The doctor smiled back. "Well, let's hope this is not too real." He looked directly at each of the companions. "Beta, Gamma, Epsilon, do you have anything you would like to add?"

The three looked at each other, as if they were silently conferring. Beta looked back to the doctor.

"As always, we are here to assist you."

Fuest nodded. "Very good. They will be here shortly. To your stations, please."

All six left quickly. Fuest found himself alone again—alone with far too many thoughts.

Maybe he could go home. Maybe he could turn the station over to others.

Maybe he should ask Vin to place himself closer to the field, in case Jon needed any help. He would have to give the young men a call.

Maybe he never needed to be alone again.

Laea thought she was all alone. She almost jumped when her younger brother came around the corner.

"What are you doing here?" Vin demanded.

"I'll stay out of the way," was the first thing she thought to say. "I know I'm supposed to be down in the records room" was the second. She stared at Vin for a second. "Aren't you supposed to be somewhere else, too?"

He grinned at that. "They couldn't keep me away either. I think I convinced them that I'm needed. I'm supposed to watch from a safe distance, and come and join the newcomers if I get the right signal from Jon."

Laea stared at the young man. "I didn't hear anything."

Vin grinned, looking at his feet. "The doctor called me. He spoke to me a few minutes after we had our meeting."

Laea thought of things she might say. In the original plans—the ones they had practiced a hundred times—the doctor thought any visitors would feel more comfortable with a human. But only one. With only four humans left on the station, they didn't want to take any unnecessary risks.

Until now.

Nobody told her anything! She was always left out, the one to be protected.

She guessed that was why she was always looking for secrets. And why she would never show her true feelings.

"What do you think they're going to do?" she said, just to say something.

"They're probably as worried about us as we are about them. Wouldn't you want to see what a new world had to offer before you started shooting it to bits?"

He led her over to the secondary hangar doors.

Two of the companions stood to either side, two of the heavy lifters, the modified soldiers. She had never seen any of them in the old hangars before. She imagined, back when ships came and went on the landing field, this type of companion often worked here. They had even stored ships in these hangars for a time. She knew from the doctor's stories that a couple of disabled vessels had been left behind in this very room. They had long ago been disassembled for parts. Now these vast rooms might once again store people and ships from other worlds. It reminded her how much things might change.

Vin saw her watching the large metal companions. Close to ten feet tall, standing between the humans and daylight, they cast huge shadows on the far wall.

"The doctor's taking no chances," he said.

This seemed to be far more complicated than she had ever imagined.

The sirens started.

"The ships are coming in." Vin pointed up into the sky, high over the heads of even the companions. "Look! There they are, flying side by side." Laea looked up, and did indeed see two small metal craft, both trailing flame from their rear engines, as they circled the landing field.

"They look like old Viper Mark Ones!" Vin was jumping up and down, no longer able to contain his excitement. "I didn't know anybody still flew that sort of thing."

Laea nodded as though she knew what he was talking about. She had heard of Vipers, but never imagined there were different types of the same craft. She had never paid that much attention to something she never imagined she would see.

"Man, look at the way they're coming down! Would I love to fly one of those things!"

The two Vipers angled sharply down, their engines silent. They were on what looked like a collision course with the science center on the far side of the field.

"They're probably trained to come in like this—fast and steep—to make a harder target."

"Target?" Laea replied blankly.

"Hey, not everyone's as welcoming as Station *Omega*. Who knows what else these guys have found out here?"

The two Vipers cut the angle of their descent, swooping just over the top of the science building to land, side by side, at the center of the strip.

The sirens stopped. Laea realized she had barely heard them in these last minutes.

"Our visitors have arrived safely." The doctor's voice came over the station's wireless. *"Let's give them a minute to look around before we go out and meet them."*

The Vipers sat there for a long moment. Laea could see waves of heat coming from the rear of each craft.

"They must still be waiting for hostile fire," Vin guessed.

"Or maybe they're talking with their ship, asking for direction. The doctor said we should give them a minute." Even Laea was getting impatient, waiting for the first sight of their visitors.

"They're opening their cockpits!" Laea saw the central section of each Viper lift away, revealing a single pilot in each craft. They paused a moment more, then both men—she was quite sure they were men—pushed themselves out of their seats and onto the wings of their craft, and from there onto the hard, paved landing field itself.

Laea realized how big this really was.

Outside of the three men on the station, these were the first people she had seen since she had been a small girl. People, new people, with more in orbit, maybe just minutes away. Two out of maybe a dozen or more—how big was their ship? Two who could take them all to see millions more, all the way back to the Colonies.

"They're holding something in their hands," Vin said, stepping closer to the window to get a look. "Are those guns?"

The two companions were instantly alert. They pressed themselves between Vin and the doorway.

"Please step away," they said in unison. "We do not wish you to be harmed."

"What's happening?"

Laea saw someone moving across the landing area. It was hard to get a good look with the two companions blocking their way.

"Where's Jon?"

"We are obeying the original protocols," the companions informed them. "We are protecting the station."

Somebody was shouting. The newcomers? They sounded frightened. She heard gunfire.

She saw more movement on the field. These new arrivals were companions, all former soldiers like the two guarding their door. The guards shifted, and she could see the humans for an instant, surrounded by others.

"No!" she shouted. This wasn't the way it was supposed to begin. They were going to talk. The ship was going to take them home. "Put down your guns! We won't hurt you!"

But she was on the far side of the door. Even if the door had been open, the two on the landing platform were much too far away to hear.

She heard another burst of gunfire, another scream. She could see nothing but a mass of companions, blocking her view of both Vipers and pilots.

She squirmed between the two guards.

"Stop it!" Laea called out as she flung open the door. "Stop it! Stop it!"

The companions didn't respond.

She had never felt so helpless.

"The Vipes are entering the atmosphere."

Griff's voice pulled the captain from his reverie, but only for an instant.

Nadu was tired of waiting. He had waited all his life.

He had said it so many times: he no longer knew what he was looking for. But when it was right, he'd feel it.

His humming grew louder. He had spent almost all his life as a raider, but for years he had only been a member of one of half a dozen crews. He remembered the day it had changed, fifteen years back.

He was crewing for the *Crusher* then, with a bunch that made the *Lightning*'s crew look a bit like gentlemen. And that was before it all fell apart.

Ah, but it had been a glorious fall. The men and women of the *Crusher* were no longer on their best behavior. They had found an ancient drug, not seen since the Cylon War.

Scavengers were never good at restraint. It would have been far better if the crew had not dipped into the supply. It would have been the height of wisdom if Nadu had not sampled it himself. He had almost lost it all to Crystal Blue.

They had found it on a moon with one lone settlement, a deserted chemical plant. Their captain at the time was overjoyed. Crystal Blue. Highly addictive, it was a license to make money. It had been outlawed on the Colonies for years, but here were barrels of the stuff—close to ten thousand doses.

Crystal Blue. Some said the Cylons created it, to drive men mad.

Crystal Blue. They were scavengers. They could take anything. Especially if you could snort it right into your system.

It was boring in space—days and days of emptiness and the cold light of distant stars. They were not disciplined like the *Lightning*'s crew. They needed something to fill the time. At first, it gave them visions. Later, it gave them pain. They only found how difficult it was to kick after nearly everyone had sampled their wares.

Their captain had tried to keep the Blue to sell back in civilization. The crew, already heavily addicted, thought otherwise. They had fought each other for the Blue, and destroyed their own ship in the process.

Thank the gods they were on the edge of the commerce lanes when the explosion had occurred. And that he had had enough sense to walk away when the glass exploded in his face. It had destroyed half his face, but the pain had pulled him away from the Blue, and forced him to think. It had saved his life. He had made it to the pod before the fire used up all the breathable air—a pod with food and water and oxygen, but not a speck of Crystal Blue.

Nadu had spent two weeks in that escape pod without the drug. Two weeks that had felt like forever, two weeks of searing pain, from the lacerations on his face and the need within his blood. He had nowhere to go, nothing to do. That was when he had first taught himself the song. The song pulled the desire from his blood and threw it out into the open air to be sucked away by the recycling units. The song pulled the need from his brain and scattered it in the space between the stars.

Crystal Blue. When he was finally rescued, he realized he could live without it. He had to live without it. Thousands and thousands of doses were destroyed with the *Crusher* and its crew. The formula was forbidden, lost in the Cylon War. There was not a day he didn't think about tasting it again. But he could stay free so long as he could sing.

The need nearly made him crazy for good. He had been crazy when he was under its spell. Sometimes he could still feel the Blue singing in his blood. Especially when they were on the edge of something. He hummed to cover up the Crystal's tune. He sang when the humming was no longer enough.

The Blue had left him with a never-ending song, a song that robbed him of sleep, but made him clever. He had found new ways to rob and cheat, new ways to finance just what he would need.

Within a year of his accident, Nadu had gone back into space with a crew of his own. A crew that his song had chosen, a crew that would complete the celestial music promised by the Blue and give Nadu all that he would ever need.

Nadu could use that idealism. It could cover up a multitude of sins.

A burst of static pulled Nadu back from his thoughts.

"Sorry, Captain," Griff said. "Having a bit of a problem getting our signals through the atmosphere. Might be a storm getting in the way." He made some adjustments to the board. "That should help. Vipes! Please repeat!"

"This is Vipes One." Twitch's voice came over the speakers, the static low behind his words. "We are making our final approach. This is quite a complex here. It's the size of a small city. We're each flying around in half a circle to see what we can see. Maybe we can get you a visual."

"I'll try to throw it on the forward screen." Griff punched a series of buttons and the screen overhead brightened. They could make out a whole series of towers rushing toward the camera. Vipes One still had its forward camera intact. Or so the theory went. But the picture didn't seem much better than the audio signal. It rolled, with bright lines flashing through the image, giving them little more than a vague sense of a city on the screen. Two many repairs on the reconditioned Vipers, Nadu guessed. Unless something was blocking their signals from below? Griff shut off the screen.

"*I've got some signs of an explosion here,*" Symm's voice cut in. "*Looks substantial, like they lost a dozen buildings. I guess this was the accident, huh?*"

"*Everything on this end looks brand new,*" Twitch added. "*Except I don't see any people. In fact, I don't think I see anybody outside at all.*"

"*They wouldn't be scared of us, would they?*" Symm said with a laugh.

Maybe the research staff was showing more sense than Nadu gave them credit for.

"Remember, boys," Griff reminded them, "they haven't seen outsiders in thirty years. They're probably scared of their own shadows."

"*We'll give them something to be afraid of, hey?*" Twitch replied.

Both the pilots laughed at that.

"We don't know what we're going to do here," Griff replied calmly. "Just because we don't see much in the way of defenses doesn't mean that they don't have any. We may actually need to negotiate to take on some cargo. We go in easy here, and polite."

"Or you'll answer to the captain!" Nadu shouted from his chair.

"*Aye, sir!*" A command from Nadu made everyone polite.

The static was getting louder again. Griff frowned as he tried to adjust the filters on his control board.

"We see the landing area. Vipes One is going in first."

"I'm circling around to join you, Twitch!"

Another burst of static, drowning a half-dozen words.

"I can see him on the ground," Symm's voice broke through. *"I'm about to follow."*

Twitch's voice followed. *"Welcome down, Symm. I see some activity, Captain. We've got a door opening at the far side of the field. I think we're going to see our hosts."*

A huge burst of static forced Griff to turn down the feed. He slowly increased the volume.

"Captain! You won't believe this!" The words were shouted through the interference. They could hear the two pilots talking but couldn't make out any more of the words.

"Ask him!" Symm demanded.

"Captain, they're not—" Twitch began.

"Oh, gods!" Symm screamed.

Twitch's voice answered. *"I'm getting out of here."*

They heard some more shouting, and then everything was drowned in the static. The Comm officer reduced the volume again. They heard no more voices.

Griff looked down at his controls. "Both Vipes are still planetside. Neither one has taken off."

"What the hell happened?" Nadu asked.

"Maybe it's time to ask our hosts." Griff keyed a new set of controls. "Research Station *Omega*! We have lost contact with our pilots. Please respond."

"Warning!" the mechanical voice announced over the speakers. *"Do not approach! We are under quarantine! Disobeying this command will result in serious consequences! Per order of the Colonial Science Protectorate!"* It was the damned tape loop, all over again! *"Warning! Do not approach! We are—"*

"I think we've just given up on the polite approach," Nadu said softly.

CHAPTER

8

Doctor Willem Fuest was beyond angry.

"How could this happen!"

"They had weapons, Doctor," Epsilon replied in its emotionless voice. "All of our models have protocols for proper procedure when weapons are involved. The protection of this station and its occupants is our primary purpose."

"It was very bad," Jon agreed. "I didn't even have a chance to get out there before they started shooting."

"Three of the companions were slightly injured in the altercation," Beta added. "All can be easily repaired. There should be no disruption of basic services."

"But what of the pilots?" the doctor demanded. "What happened to them?"

It was Gamma's turn to talk. "The pilots were subdued. They were slightly damaged, but nothing happened to them that would be life-threatening."

"So we may be able to get out of this after all. We don't know who these people are or what kind of firepower they have at their disposal. I was hoping—at best—for an exchange of ideas, and maybe a chance to send a message home. I did not expect a war." He turned to Epsilon. "Now where are the prisoners? I need to talk to them at once!"

"It may take a short time before—" the warrior model began.

"Doctor!" Vin called from the far side of the room. "We have a new wireless communication from the *Lightning!*"

"I had best respond to this." The doctor looked at all three companions. "Make certain the prisoners are kept as comfortable as possible. If we can give them back to the *Lightning*, perhaps we can save this visit."

He was never good under pressure. Somehow, if he didn't want more bloodshed, he would have to rise to the occasion. *Oh, Betti*, he thought. *If only I had your way with words.*

"Let's hear what the *Lightning* has to say," he said to Vin.

Griff didn't like this one bit. He opened the same wireless channel he had used before.

The research station might be broadcasting that repeating garbage, but that didn't mean they couldn't receive a signal.

"Station *Omega*. We have lost contact with our pilots. Where are our pilots?"

He knew the look on his captain's face. He'd initiated

this contact on his own. This wouldn't be the first time he had kept Nadu from killing everyone in sight.

"Station *Omega*. This is Cruiser *Lightning*. Repeat. We have lost contact with our pilots. Respond, or we will take retaliatory action."

Nadu stared at him. "You actually expect them to have some frakking response?" He waved to others on deck. "Load the forward missiles. They'll get more polite once we've blown up a building or two."

Griff ignored his captain, still trying for a response. "Station *Omega*. If we do not receive a response, we will consider this an act of war. You will be fired upon."

The warning loop, which Griff had kept playing faintly in the background, cut out abruptly. Griff turned up the volume on the incoming feed.

"*Cruiser* Lightning, *this is Station* Omega." The familiar voice of the doctor cut through the static. "*Our apologies. I'm afraid we've had a little misunderstanding.*"

Well, that was a polite way to put it. Griff replied, "Station, we want to speak to our pilots. Now."

"*Cruiser* Lightning. *Those were fighters you sent down. Our defense protocols are a little primitive, I'm afraid. They have a programmed response to any ships that might pose a threat. Your pilots and their ships were both . . . neutralized before I could intervene. But no harm has come to your pilots or their ships.*"

Griff glanced at Nadu. The captain glared back without response. That was Griff's job now.

"If our pilots are unharmed, we need to speak to them."

It took the doctor a moment to respond. *"I'm sure you can, in a short time. I'll have to get them patched into our wireless network. They are being held in a separate facility. When last I saw them, they were quite incoherent."*

"What have they got down there?" Nadu asked softly. Griff knew exactly what he was thinking. Symm and Twitch were usually ready to take on a dozen armed men with their bare hands.

Griff opened the wireless channel again.

"What aren't you telling us, *Omega*? We have a full complement of weapons. If we suspect any foul play, we will not hesitate to use them."

Another moment of silence.

"Oh dear," the doctor's voice finally replied. *"That would be most distressing. There are other matters I need to bring up to you, about our companions. I think your men had a reaction—"*

Griff cut him off. He didn't have the time to listen to the doctor's ramblings. "Let us talk to our pilots, and we can work this out. Otherwise . . ." Griff let the rest of the sentence hang.

"No, no. Please, you told me you'd send somebody a bit more—diplomatic. That was your term, wasn't it? I'm sure we can work everything out. Now that I've seen the protocols, I can shut them down. The same thing won't happen twice, I assure you. I'll meet the next transport personally."

Griff glanced at the captain again. This time, Nadu nodded his agreement. It was Griff's call, then.

"Very well. We'll send down a team of three in a landing transport. You'll be talking with a young man who has my full confidence—Tom Zarek."

"No," the captain cut in loudly. "We will also send an escort. Two more Vipers, prepared to blast your station to rubble at the first sign of anything questionable. Do you understand?"

"*Understood.*" The doctor paused, then added, "*I really don't think—*"

Griff cut him off mid-sentence. "We will want them to see the pilots first. As soon as our transport lands. Do you agree?"

The doctor paused a moment before answering again. "*I'm—I'm sure we'll work everything out.*" He sounded overwhelmed.

Griff almost felt sorry for the doctor. "No doubt. You're here alone on the edge of space. I imagine you can't be too careful, hey? Do you agree?"

"*I'll make sure the pilots are ready to talk. If you could give me a little time—*"

"Our diplomatic mission will meet you very shortly. We are quite concerned about the health of our men. I'm sure you understand. I will open a channel again when we launch the transport. Please be ready. Cruiser *Lightning* out."

Griff cut the connection. He looked up to the captain. "So?"

"You didn't give him a choice," Nadu answered with the slightest of smiles. "We'll get our men. Maybe we can get them without too many of their people being killed."

Griff still didn't have the best feeling about all of this.

"What do you make of this doctor who seems to run things?"

The captain shook his head. "He doesn't run things very well."

"He sounds a bit like a fool," Griff agreed. "Or someone in way over his head."

"He may lack experience in this. It would take a certain amount of brains and guts to work on a station way out here. I don't know exactly who we are dealing with here, but I do not think they are fools."

Griff thought the captain was right. This might not be quite so easy a jaunt as they had thought.

"Maybe they're just being cautious," he suggested. "Maybe they're planning to use our pilots as hostages to force our good behavior."

Nadu let out a short bark of a laugh. "Let's hope it's that interesting. It would amuse me to do a little negotiating."

It was Griff's turn to laugh. Last time somebody tried to bargain with him, the captain had finished the negotiated exchange and then promptly shot everyone on the other side.

"I agree with you," Nadu added abruptly. "Zarek's best for the job."

"Out of our available talent?" Griff shrugged. "He's young. He can think on his feet. He's expendable."

"It's the first law of scavengers. With great risks come great rewards. Besides, we haven't really even broken him in."

Compared with most of those on board, Zarek was

barely a part of the crew. And there were always other young men looking for opportunity.

This would be his first test. Tom was a survivor. He would find his way through this. Griff would be surprised if young Zarek didn't outlast them all.

Captain Nadu started his tuneless humming once more, then abruptly stopped. "We'll send him out on his peace mission. And we'll get the rest of them ready for war."

He waved at Griff.

"Call another general meeting. I think we need to build a little fire underneath our crew."

CHAPTER

9

FREE CRUISER *LIGHTNING*

Before this, Tom Zarek realized, he had never seen his captain truly angry.

Nadu's scarred face seemed to glow in the subdued light of the control room, his cross-hatched flesh twitching with a ruined energy.

Zarek had barely gotten back to his bunk before they had sounded another "all hands." The remaining crew had all scrambled back to the control center. Griff had singled him out, and told him to step forward and stand by the comm station.

Griff scanned the room, silently counting the crewmembers. "We're all here, then? I'm afraid we have a bit of a problem." He nodded to the captain. Nadu paced about his station at the center of the room, glaring first at one cluster of the crew, then another, so that his good eye had scanned all of them in turn.

No one else spoke. They all knew when not to cross their captain.

"They have captured Symm and Twitch." Nadu grimaced, as though just saying the words brought him pain. "Well, they *say* they are being detained. They give me double talk about problems with their defenses."

He turned and slammed his fist down on the control console before him.

"They want to play Nadu for a fool." His tone said that was a mistake. "They say they have technical difficulties!" His voice was rising with every sentence. He stopped to take a ragged breath.

"They're trying to keep us in the dark," Griff said into the silence. "They have their own agenda."

Nadu turned to stare at the comm officer, clenching and unclenching the fist that he had so recently slammed into his controls. Zarek realized his knuckles were bleeding.

"My second in command makes a valid point," Nadu said softly. He looked like he would kill Griff anyway. "Perhaps we should drop a few missiles to light our way."

"That would jeopardize our pilots," Griff replied in equally measured tones. "Our men are in their hands. We hope for their sake that they are still alive. They claim they have made a mistake."

When Nadu didn't reply, he added, "At least they are still talking to us."

Griff looked out to the assembled crew. "The rest of

you did not witness our pilots' landing. It's quite a facility they have down there. But at the very last minute, we lost our visual feed. We heard a few shots fired."

"Shots?" asked Grets, the woman who acted as both ship's cook and doctor.

"A few," Griff replied. "No prolonged gun battles. We pray they were not executed."

"That would be a foolish thing to do. Let us hope they were just detained. We would not want them to be lying to us." Nadu smiled broadly. It was a frightening sight. "I will now tell you all what we will do."

Nadu paused to look at every single person in the room. "We have men missing. We never have men unaccounted for. We will find our missing pilots. And if our new friends have done anything to our pilots, they will be very sorry. They do not frak with Nadu!" He pounded his bloody hand on a second console, grunting with the pain.

"We are to assume—until they convince us otherwise—that the inhabitants of this place are not to be trusted."

The ship was full of stories of how Nadu had outwitted another bunch of scavengers, or traders, or even whole Colonies. Maybe, Zarek realized, this was why the captain was so angry. The stories always had a common thread—how Nadu would say one thing and plot another. It was almost as if Nadu were looking in a mirror. He had had his own double-dealing techniques used against him.

"But, if they are to be believed, we are the first outsiders they have seen in decades. They need us, for supplies, for news from home." He smiled again. "Maybe they're even looking for a way back home! We will use everything we can to bargain."

"Five of you will be going down," Griff said. "We're calling this a peace mission. You will give them a chance to explain their actions. And remember, any shooting could damage potentially lucrative merchandise."

"Exactly," Nadu agreed. "But if anyone makes a move against you, feel free to kill them."

"Perhaps we should locate our pilots before we get too aggressive," Griff replied.

Nadu stared at his second in command. "Perhaps."

"Five are going," Griff repeated.

"We need someone who can think on his feet." Nadu pointed at Tom. "Zarek. You can talk as well as anyone. I'm putting this second landing under your control. But watch everything."

So that was why he had been asked to step forward. This was the first time he'd been entrusted with anything of importance. He had tagged along on a few exploratory missions, and Griff would let him fill in on the comm board in off-hours, but until now he thought that Nadu barely knew his name.

"Yes, sir," he managed.

"Get our men back. That's your primary goal. Then you can talk to the people down at the station, see what they want. See what they have to offer. Oh, and see what they're trying to keep for themselves. Don't promise them a thing. For anything final, you have to talk to me."

"Yes sir."

"We'll keep a channel open with the lander. If any questions—or any difficulties—arise, there'll be somebody on the other end you can talk to."

"Sounds good, sir."

Nadu actually clapped him on the shoulder.

"Zarek, if you do well on this, you'll get a bonus." The captain smiled. "If not—well, no one will miss a junior member of the crew."

Nadu pointed at different members of the crowd. "You'll take the lander. And bring the Creep along. You and you will pilot the escort."

"Remember, I want seven of you back here." He looked at everyone crammed into the corners of the room.

"The rest of you are dismissed."

Zarek saw flashes of relief on the others' faces. Nobody expected this was going to be an easy ride.

But this was what he had signed up for. If he handled this well, he might get the sort of reward he was looking to get out of this.

He watched the crew retreat through the hatches. Tom realized he didn't know exactly who else was on the mission until the crowd thinned out. Well, everybody knew the Creep, a tall, skinny man who seldom spoke and always dressed in gray. They said he could get in and out of anything before the other guys knew he was there. That's why he had the name.

It grew very quiet. The control center had emptied of all but the senior staff and the five going out. Zarek could hear the soft mechanical pings and whirs of the various boards that managed the ship. He nodded to the other men who would go out with him on the mission. Their pilot would be Boone—he generally took out the larger ships. He was an affable guy, always willing to show Zarek the ropes. Tom would be glad to have him along. Slam and Ajay would be escorting them down in the old Mark One Vipers. Zarek liked both of them better than the two idiots—Symm and Twitch—that bunked across from him. He wondered if they would ever really get them back, and realized he didn't miss those two in the least.

The replacement Viper pilots were both fairly new on the crew. Zarek thought Ajay had logged only a couple more months here than he had. Maybe they hadn't had time yet to grow into proper idiots.

Griff talked to them first. "We expect you to pay attention down there. This is the most—" He paused to search for the word. "—rewarding job we've had in a long time. This could be a big payday if we handle it right."

"You'll be taking weapons." Nadu spread his arms wide. "Big guns, which I expect you to wave around a bit. They bring us Twitch and Symm, we'll make nice. Until then, watch your step."

Zarek realized that, with two crewmen going down the first time and five down the second, the captain was committing almost half his crew to this venture. Nadu wouldn't be turning back from this one. One way or another, he would get his payday.

"Any questions?" Griff asked.

Nobody dared to ask anything.

"We've got two of our own to rescue," Nadu announced. "I want you out of here now." With that, he returned to his command console. As if he didn't want to see them again until the job was done.

Tom Zarek left with the others. All five went straight up to the launch bay.

Boone looked to the storage lockers that surrounded the bay. "Let's take anything we think we can use. Guns, grenades, survival gear. I'm going to take seven suits in the lander. If we have to, we'll cram everyone in together to get back here."

The lander was large enough to normally seat five. It carried atmosphere suits and rations to last a full crew for two weeks. It was as close to an escape vehicle as the *Lightning* had. What would Nadu do if they didn't come back? If it came to that, Tom imagined the captain would crash the *Lightning* into the research station, killing the rest of the crew just to get back at whoever crossed him on this planet.

And how did Tom feel about this? He couldn't afford feelings. He was in this until the end.

Boone and the Creep loaded their arms with whatever weapons they found to hand. Zarek grabbed an extra pair of suits—with their bulk, two suits was all he could manage. Boone climbed in through the hatch and told the others to pass him everything. No one else entered his boat until he had everything in place.

Boone popped his head back out after a moment. "We still got some room." He waved at the pilots. "Ajay. Bring me a couple of extra cases of rations. That sort of thing has trading value."

The Vipes pilot frowned as he lifted the supplies. "Shouldn't we ask someone before we take all of this?"

"Do you want to talk to the captain again? Besides, if its down here, it's surplus. It means the stores up in the galley are full."

Boone took the cases from the pilot and disappeared inside.

"Almost ready," he said when he appeared again. "One more thing." He pointed into the far corner of the room. "Zarek, open the locker all the way down on the left."

Zarek went over and tried the locker door. It was stuck.

"Kick it a couple times!" Boone called. "Can't have people getting at it too easy. It's my own private stash."

Zarek banged the bottom of the locker with his boot. The metal door swung free. The locker was mostly empty, with only a small, ornately carved box on an upper shelf, while a battered case, stenciled with the words PROPERTY OF THE COLONIAL FORCES, lay at the bottom.

"See that case?" Boone asked loudly. "Bring it along."

Zarek pulled the case out of the locker. It was surprisingly heavy. He half carried, half dragged it over to the lander.

"It's an old survival kit we scavenged from our last stop," Boone explained as he waited. "I think it predates the war."

Tom hefted the case up to the hatch with a grunt. Boone wrestled it inside.

"We're looking for anything that will give us an

edge." Boone continued to talk as he disappeared inside. "And, seeing how we have no idea what we're getting into, we're looking for anything. I figure an extra case of emergency gear can't hurt."

Zarek realized Boone was the one with the real experience around here. Why hadn't Nadu made him the leader of the expedition? Zarek was a fast talker, but he didn't have one tenth of Boone's savvy.

"Okay," Boone announced as he once again appeared. "I've got everything nailed down. You guys can come on in." He took a step back to let them in. "Let's do a quick check of our systems and get the frak on our way. The sooner we're out of the captain's sight, the better."

The Creep was first, sliding in front of Zarek before Tom could react. Zarek supposed the Creep would be a good man to have on his side. And, since he never talked, Tom could ignore him when he didn't need him.

He climbed into the lander last, and strapped himself into the copilot's seat. He liked to watch Boone at work. The pilot moved the lander up and down like it was just an extra pair of legs. He could put the pear-shaped vessel just about anywhere and not break a sweat.

He saw that the Creep was already in place. Sitting in the back, where he could watch everybody and everything. The Creep nodded when Zarek looked his way. Tom nodded back. It was the most communication he had ever had with the guy. Some people just really earned their nicknames.

Boone flipped the switch on the small wireless control in front of Zarek. "Lander to Vipes. Are you receiving?"

"Vipes Three, okay," came back.

"Vipes Four?" Boone asked. "Are you receiving?"

He got a burst of static. A voice cut in with a string of curse words. *"Oh!"* Ajay's voice remarked. *"I've got it now. Vipes Four, okay."*

Boone let out a heavy sigh. "You know, Tom, I have a dream. And in this dream I'm on a ship where everything works."

He laughed softly as he gently patted the controls in front of him.

"Guess it's good that's just a dream, huh? Well, we know this baby will get us there and back."

He flipped a dozen switches in order, three rows of four. "Wherever we're going, Vara will get us there."

Vara was Boone's own private name for the landing ship. Zarek grinned. Boone only used it around people he trusted.

Boone hit the comm control. "Command Center. This is Boone. All three ships are ready for deployment."

"This is Command," Griff's voice replied. *"You are cleared for takeoff."*

"Copy that, Control. Vipes Three. Vipes Four. We're going out. At two-minute intervals. Vipes first, Three then Four. The lander here will follow. Understood?"

"Understood and ready to roll."

Another burst of static. *"Understood! I can hear you fine."* Ajay cursed again. *"I'll just have to hit my wireless a few times if I need to talk back."*

"Perfect conditions, as usual." Boone shook his head. "Command Center, do you read? We are ready to begin the mission."

"*Acknowledge, Lander One,*" Griff's voice came back to them.

"Ready for launch," Boone replied. "Viper Three, Viper Four, Lander."

"*We copy your launch pattern. Launch pattern okay.*"

"*Get the frakkers!*" Nadu shouted in the background.

"Yes sir, Captain!" Boone replied. "Vipes Three, away!"

Zarek could feel the deck shake as the first Viper left its launchpad. The lander had a pair of larger windows, but they were both behind his seat, and a smaller window up front, between the dradis screen and the controls. But he was focused on Boone as the pilot got them off the ground.

A light in front of them changed from orange to white.

"Vipes Four, away!" Boone ordered.

The deck rumbled again.

Boone looked over at Zarek. "Brace yourself, Tom. We're going on a little adventure."

He watched Boone work the switches and dials, easing just a bit of force from the thrusters as he pulled back on the joystick. Early on, Zarek had flown a mission with Boone and had marveled at the way the pilot had smoothly and effortlessly maneuvered the lander. When Zarek told him what he thought, Boone had laughed, talking about how you had to know just what Vara

101

needed. He had offered to give the younger man a few lessons when they could find the time. But both men had gotten busy in the weeks that followed, checking out their captain's "hunches"—wild ideas, that, Tom now realized, often led nowhere.

He actually half wished he had asked again about the offered lessons. Maybe, after all this was over, he'd find a way to make the time. In the meantime, he supposed he would just sit back and watch a master at work.

Captain Nadu and his hunches. Zarek thought about watching the two men in charge back in the Command Center. He could really see the way the two of them played off each other, Nadu reaching for the stratosphere, Griff hauling him back down. Whatever worked, he supposed. Nadu might be a little crazy, but the *Lightning* was well known as one of the richest scavenging crews around.

The lights changed again on the display before them.

"Lander One, away!" Boone called as he punched the thrusters, pushing the ship quickly down the launch chute and out into space.

"Well, that's it for a bit. When I get to the atmosphere, I'll give our hosts a call. I thought I'd get us off the ship. But you heard the captain. Once we land, Tom, it's all your show." He waved at the weapons, everything from handguns to what looked like a small cannon, which he had strapped against the walls. "They assure us everything will be fine. Nothing to worry about, hey boys?"

Tom tried to reply with a small laugh, but nothing much came out. The Creep was silent.

Boone checked his instruments. "One Research Station *Omega*, dead ahead. I don't even have to turn this thing. We'll settle down, gentle as a falling leaf."

Zarek was feeling confined by his chair. He turned to the pilot. "Mind if I take a walk?"

Boone grinned. "Go as far as you like. Nothing else we can do for a little while."

Zarek unbuckled his belt and rose from his seat. He looked around the craft as they pushed their way through space toward the planet below.

Unlike the Vipers, the lander had very limited armaments. Most landers of this type had none, but Nadu had customized Boone's Vara a bit by adding a couple of small guns with rapidly repeating fire, each gun positioned immediately below one of the lander's two windows. Zarek didn't think the captain was comfortable without everything having a couple of extra guns. The lander was designed for short hops planetside and had plenty of room for cargo, both below decks and here, where Boone had managed to secure anything they might need very close at hand. If something went bad, they did not lack for firepower.

Their wireless squawked to life. *"This is Research Station* Omega. *We detect three ships on our instruments. Are you the new party from the* Lightning?*"*

"And who else might we be?" Boone asked before he hit the reply switch.

"We are the new party," Boone replied, once he had turned on his mic. "One lander with a two-Viper escort."

"*I see,*" the voice responded. Then nothing for a minute. "*We wish you could have waited a bit, so we could be a bit more prepared. I'm afraid we aren't much at protocol.*" Another pause. "*Your pilots are fine. We do appreciate your concern. Once you have landed, we will explain everything.*"

Boone raised his eyebrows and looked over at Zarek. This, Tom guessed, is my cue.

He took over the microphone.

"This is Tom Zarek. I'm the one you'll be talking with. We want to clear this up just as much as you do, I assure you. Give us our pilots and we'll just chalk this up to a misunderstanding. Maybe we can find something to trade. We can start over again, and find business that's mutually beneficial."

"*Thank you, Mr. Zarek. I am Doctor Fuest. I am sure, once you have seen our facility, that we can find much to talk about. Despite our earlier problems, I assure you we want nothing but positive results from our contact.*"

He paused, then added, "*I look forward to meeting you.*" Another pause before he added, "*Please wait by your ships. And don't be surprised by what you see. Appearances can be deceiving.*"

The signal went dead. Zarek stared at the apparatus before him.

"Maybe they're not used to talking on the wireless."

"It doesn't sound like they're very happy to see us," Boone added after a moment's thought. "It sounds like they're going to cross us all over again. Or maybe we've both spent far too much time with Captain Nadu."

They all laughed at that, even the Creep, more to release tension than to share any real humor.

"But they're letting us land," Tom said after another moment had passed. "I think I've calmed them down."

"You did that," Boone agreed. "I can see why they picked you to lead the mission. Even I believed what you were saying."

Zarek thought that Boone was the real leader here—the guy with the experience. He was only the front man—the vocal chords of the operation.

"Well, maybe we can find something of value without having to shoot anyone," Zarek said, not even believing the words himself. "We'll have to wait and see."

The pilot glanced up at his readouts.

"We are now entering planetary atmosphere," Boone announced. "We'll be down shortly." He glanced back at Zarek. "You'd better strap yourself in, Tom. We'll be hitting turbulence in a second."

Zarek nodded and strapped himself in next to the Creep, so he could look through the windows.

That was the last of their conversation.

Now that their destination was set, none of them wanted to talk. They were surrounded by the silence. Zarek watched the small disk of the planet grow through the portal, a patchwork of green and blue, not that different from his home world, Caprica.

The planet looked so peaceful. It looked like a place

that would take easily to colonization. But only one small corner of the whole world had been touched, a gleaming silver city stuck between endless green jungle and deep blue sea.

He felt he couldn't breathe the air on Caprica. He had had to escape. Space was vast, and all around them. But instead of being trapped in an apartment in a city on a civilized world, he found himself in a tiny metal box smaller than any room he had ever lived in, crammed with people and supplies, on the wild fringes of space where there were no rules at all. Flying between the stars mostly made him want to walk again on solid ground.

Well, Zarek had always known this *Lightning* job was a short-term solution. There had to be something better after his run with scavengers. After this, he would do something that would make a difference, and make a name for Tom Zarek.

If he lived to see the end of this voyage.

He thought about the captain's mention of weapons fire. It was a sound, nothing more. Had it come from the Vipes pilots, the research station, or both?

The research station didn't trust them—quite wisely. He would expect them to arm themselves. And he had to find a way to keep them from using those weapons.

"Time to go to the party," Boone said into the silence. He hit a switch on the wireless.

"Research Station *Omega*. This is the landing party from *Lightning*, requesting permission to land."

He closed the channel and grinned back at the others. "As if they could do anything else."

"Permission granted," a voice said from the station. *"Approaching craft! I repeat, please remain with your ships after landing. A party will come out to the landing platform to meet you. We had an unfortunate situation with your fellow crewmen. Please do not judge us before we have a chance to explain."*

Zarek did not find any of this reassuring. He looked to Boone and the Creep. "I've been thinking. Maybe we shouldn't show the guns right away. We don't know what—or who—we're dealing with."

Nobody raised any objection.

"Keep the guns close," he continued. "But the captain said I should be diplomatic. So, before we do anything else, I'll try to talk them into giving us our guys." He thought again how he'd be just as happy if he never saw either of the Vipes pilots ever again.

"And maybe we can get them to give us a few other things, too."

The Creep spoke at last. "We'll let you make your statement. But where's the fun in cooperation? When I've got a gun, I like to use it." He shrugged as he looked at a rifle secured by his feet. "Maybe I can shoot a few of them on the way out."

"No, no, we got it," Boone assured Tom. "Talk first, shoot later. Pretty simple, huh?"

Zarek only wished it were.

Boone switched on the wireless.

"Research Station *Omega*. We're coming in."

CHAPTER

10

RESEARCH STATION *OMEGA*

Zarek watched as the two Vipers set down one after another on the empty expanse of the landing pad. He saw no signs of the earlier Vipers, or their pilots. Could they have been dragged into the large building at the far end of the field? Why, if the authorities here were going to return the pilots, had they gotten rid of their spacecraft?

The landing field, in fact, showed no signs of life at all. From the air, the station looked deserted, with whole parts of it in ruins. The landing field, though, was in perfect shape, with dark painted grids to help guide in ships from space. Ships they said they hadn't seen in years.

He supposed this was all the welcome they would get. What did he expect—"Welcome *Lightning*" banners?

Tom felt a tightness in his chest. He had to go out and meet these people, to smile one minute and be ready to shoot the next. Oh well. He guessed it would be good training in case he ever went into politics.

His jokes weren't helping his nerves. This was the first time, he realized, that he had been given actual authority. He wondered, absently, what his father would say about Tom if his son ever made something of himself, after all the times the old man had called him a failure? Would his father even recognize him?

And would it even matter?

Both the Vipers were down, each taxiing across the landing field, turning slightly, angling across the field, to leave a wide space between them. A space for Boone to land, so that the Vipers would have a clear shot if the locals tried anything.

Only now did Tom realize he hadn't spoken to his father in years. Bits of the life he thought he had left behind came back to him: fights with his father, mostly; the day he decided never to return to the university, he remembered that one well. But later things, too: his abortive attempt to get the kitchen workers to stand up to management; getting thrown out of his lodgings because he could no longer pay; the woman he'd met who knew a man who knew somebody that crewed for the *Lightning*. How young he seemed in all those memories.

He was a different person now. A better person. And he was going to survive this and more. He couldn't afford any doubts. His stint on the *Lightning* was going to send him on his way. He was going to end up richer than his wildest dreams.

Unless, of course, he ended up dead. Nadu had

been quick to point out that everyone in the crew was expendable.

"Here we go into the fire," Boone said softly as he lowered his lander. He maneuvered the craft so that it swung in low, midway between the Vipes, then let it touch down and roll to a stop with barely a bump. The man was an artist.

Boone and the Creep both checked their weapons. Tom supposed he had better do the same. Both of the others carried big guns with rapid-repeat firepower; they could unload their hundred-shot magazines in little more than a minute. He carried only a sidearm—a pistol with a dozen shots. He was the peacemaker, after all. He planned to keep the sidearm under his coat, and pull it out only if things went very bad indeed. He lifted the gun and took mock aim at the hatch. The sidearm felt much heavier than he remembered it. Perhaps it was the planet's gravity. This world was close to the size of Caprica, while the ship's grav was usually set to Picon-normal—about eighty-five percent of what they'd find here. Or maybe the gun would always feel heavy with the potential targets waiting just outside.

He knew how to use this—he'd spent hours on simulated target practice down in *Lightning*'s cargo hold. He wondered what would happen when and if he had to shoot another human being.

He looked out the nearest portal. No one had emerged from any of the buildings to greet them. The field looked just as deserted as it had from the air.

What were the research people up to? Who knew

what kind of weapons they hid in these buildings. Nadu's decisions didn't always follow the strict dictates of logic, but right now, this felt downright suicidal.

"If they're not going to talk to us, maybe we'd better talk among ourselves." Boone opened a wireless channel. "This is a secure channel. We're ready here. Vipes report your status."

"Vipes Three ready," came back immediately.

They waited a moment, but heard nothing from Vipes Four.

"Ajay's still having trouble sending, I guess." Boone spoke into the mic. "Vipes. We're facing the unknown here. Tom thinks it would be a good idea to keep our weapons out of sight."

Zarek leaned forward to explain.

"Everybody!" he began clearly. "No matter what you see, unless we see a gun pointed at us, we don't raise our own. We keep them ready, but we do not use them until I give the signal. Our first priority is to retrieve the prisoners. We want to get everybody out of here in one piece—and alive."

"Do you copy, Vipes?" Boone added.

"Vipes Three, copy."

This time, they heard a second burst of static. Vipes Four's answer?

They could only hope that Ajay was still receiving their signal.

"We've got a door opening!" the Creep called from his station by a window. "Three figures are coming out and walking toward us. Frak!"

"What's the matter?" Zarek asked. "Do they have weapons?"

The Creep glanced back at them. He looked even more pale than usual. "No weapons that I can see. But two of them aren't human."

"What?" Both Zarek and Boone moved across the lander to get a look.

"It can't be," Boone whispered.

But it was. A tall thin human walked between two machines—machines that looked like Cylons. They weren't the models used as warriors—seeing the military, Centurion Cylons would be as good as seeing a loaded gun. Zarek had been very young when the Cylons had left, but even he recognized that these were both domestic models—a Cylon Butler, maybe, and a Cylon Mechanic.

"I think Nadu needs to know about this." Boone moved quickly back to the wireless.

"Do we get the frak away from here?" the Creep whispered.

"And leave the pilots behind?" Boone called over his shoulder. "Nadu would have our skins."

"But—" the Creep began, but let his objections die. They all knew that, with Nadu, there were no extenuating circumstances.

Zarek tried to make sense of what he saw. At the end of the war, the Cylons had left for who knew where. Could it be that, when *Lightning* came to this outpost, they had actually found the edge of Cylon-controlled space? But then why would a human be walking with them? No, this was something new, something to do with this special research station.

Did their research here, far away from any civilized worlds, have to do with taming their former enemies? Or had the war completely passed this place by?

Zarek couldn't judge anything by appearances. Humans and Cylons, side by side. He felt like he was stepping back into history.

Boone came up behind him. "I sent a coded message out to the captain telling him we've got something strange. Something that looks like Cylons."

"No reply?"

"None yet. The last Vipers down here had their signal break up, didn't they? Some sort of atmospheric interference, maybe."

"Or maybe someone is jamming the signal." Tom nodded. He realized he didn't trust anything about this anymore. But he still had to finish his job. "Keep this ship ready to take off. I'm going to step outside. I think, if we want any hope of getting Symm and Twitch, we've got to show ourselves. But I don't want anybody more than a step or two away from his craft."

Boone returned to his station to tell the others.

"Vipes! We're going ahead with the meet. Tom will go out first. Then we'll all show ourselves. If possible, we'll negotiate for our pilots. If not—remember, wait for Tom's signal."

"When I wave both hands above my head," Zarek called over his shoulder, "get back in your flyers and go."

Both Zarek and Boone went to look out the portal.

The Creep was right behind them. The three-member welcoming committee was halfway across the field.

"They told us not to judge by appearances," Tom said softly.

"Cylon technology might be worth a lot," the Creep added. "Didn't the toasters take almost all of it with them?"

"We're here just long enough to get Twitch and Symm," Tom said. "I think any other talk will happen later."

"Maybe we can send Nadu down instead," the Creep suggested.

Boone glanced at Zarek. "Yeah, I guess you've convinced us to stay. I really wish our captain was a little less crazy."

Tom nodded. "Open the hatch, Boone."

The pilot flipped the lever. The hatch popped open with a hiss.

Tom stepped out of the lander. What did you say to a man and two Cylons?

Viper Three popped open its cockpit. Slam stood up in the craft, his hands empty.

Tom saw no movement from the other Viper. But the three locals were well within hailing distance.

"Greetings!" he said in a loud, clear voice. "I'm Tom Zarek, from the independent cruiser *Lightning*. We're glad to finally meet you."

The man and the two Cylons stopped, maybe twenty paces away.

Tom walked forward slowly, putting some distance

between himself and the lander. Behind him, he could see that both his crewmates had stepped just beyond the hatch, showing themselves to be empty-handed, but keeping their weapons within arm's reach.

Zarek could finally get a good look at the human in the center. He was a very thin, aged gentleman who held himself quite straight, in an almost military posture.

"You are Doctor Fuest?" Zarek asked as he continued to approach the three others.

"I am." The old man stared at him. He did not smile. "And I want to thank you first for not overreacting."

Zarek nodded to the mechanicals who flanked the old man. "I have to admit, I did not expect your friends."

Fuest nodded at that, and finally smiled. Mention of the Cylons, oddly, seemed to put him a bit more at ease. He waved at his metal escort. "I would wonder if anything like this exists anymore, back in the Colonies. We work with our friends here—or, as we call them, our companions. I know, they remind you of certain mechanical servants the Colonies once employed, but our society here is far different, perhaps unique in all of known space—if you knew these companions well, you would not be so afraid."

Was it that obvious? Zarek thought he had been hiding his emotions. He glanced around the landing area. The rest of the field still seemed empty. It certainly was strange, but no one had threatened them—yet.

But two people were missing here. Seeing the Cylons had thrown him off.

"We are here to receive our prisoners!" he called.

"Very well," the doctor called. "I will have them brought out. I want nothing but for this exchange to succeed."

So they would get Symm and Twitch? Perhaps he should take the final steps forward and greet the doctor more properly. Zarek smiled, and extended his hand.

"On behalf of the *Lightning*—" he began.

One of the Cylons—the Butler—stepped forward to block Tom's way.

Zarek heard a shout. He turned as the final Vipes popped its top.

Ajay came out screaming.

"The Cylons run this place. They're everywhere. Get back! Get back! Get away from here!"

Boone shouted behind him. Zarek turned, and saw something silver moving across the field.

Ajay had a gun. He pulled out his machine rifle and started shooting.

"No!" Zarek shouted, but his protest was lost beneath the gunfire.

Doors flew open in the buildings to either side. Plates drew back on the landing field to show Cylons hidden beneath. And not just domestics. Zarek recognized those barrel bodies and snakelike arms. These were Centurions. They leapt from their hiding places, weapons aimed and ready.

Ajay was right. The real Cylons were now everywhere.

Fuest was shouting something, too, but Zarek couldn't hear it. He lifted his arms above his head—the signal to abort the mission.

No one was watching him anymore. It happened too quickly. The crew of the *Lightning* had been fired upon, and they were fighting back.

But only four crewmembers were firing guns. The Cylons seemed endless. Slam tumbled out of his cockpit as bullets ripped across his chest. Ajay's mouth opened as a bullet opened the back of his brain. Zarek looked back and saw that one of Boone's pants legs was drenched in blood. Both Boone and the Creep were hunched down low, using the lander for cover.

Maybe, Zarek thought, if he could get back to the lander, the three of them might still get away.

He realized no one was firing at him. No bullets flew around the group at the center of the field. Zarek was being protected by his proximity to Doctor Fuest.

He jumped forward, dodging the Butler, who now looked past him at the gunfire. Zarek could finally hear the doctor's voice.

"Stop it!" Fuest called to the Cylons at either side. When he saw Tom approach he shouted, "I don't want this any more than you."

Zarek saw one of the doctor's guardians out of the corner of his eye. The repair Cylon's wrenchlike hands reached for his throat. Tom ducked and rolled, straight toward the doctor's feet.

Zarek realized he had only one way out of this. He jumped up behind the doctor, pinning the old man's arms against his chest. Fuest was very thin, almost frail. Zarek lifted him off the ground and backed away, using the doctor as a shield.

Fuest didn't struggle. "What are you doing?" the doctor called over his shoulder.

"If I don't do this, I'm dead," Zarek shot back.

Fuest shook his head. "No, no, the companions will listen to me. I can stop them."

"Like they're listening to you now?"

"It was working so well before you came. I can't understand . . ." The doctor's voice trailed off as his two guardians rushed to follow Tom.

"Stay back!" Fuest called to the machines. "We can find some reason here!"

The machines didn't seem to listen.

"This can't be happening," the doctor mumbled. "This can't be happening."

Now Fuest was the one who looked really afraid.

Zarek backed up, with the old man stumbling after him.

He could hear the whine of gunfire in his ears. Boone and the Creep seemed to be holding their own against the Cylons. Zarek flinched as a shot buzzed past his head. A couple of the bullets were close, but for some reason, the Cylons seemed to value the doctor.

Maybe he was right, Tom thought, and these "companions" of his were different. Maybe they were slightly more selective killing machines.

The gunfire stopped abruptly as Tom reached the lander.

Boone looked up at him from where the pilot crouched against the ship. "Do you think we've given them enough chance to talk?"

Zarek nodded to the doctor. "I've brought a little protection with us. They don't want him hurt. Maybe we can talk to him after we've loaded all of us back on the lander."

Boone grinned. "That's why Nadu picked you to be the leader."

"Hey, it never hurts to have a hostage," the Creep agreed. "Watch out!"

Zarek turned, and realized the Cylons had stopped firing so that they could close in on foot. Half a dozen of the things towered over them. Boone rolled onto his back and shot one of the Centurions point blank, severing its head from its neck. But a pair of Cylons pushed past their fallen comrade. Four arms came down on Boone's body, knocking the gun from his hands and crushing his chest. Other arms were pulling the doctor from Zarek's grip. Still holding onto the old man, he used the Cylon's weight to swing himself around toward the lander, diving through the hatch.

"Creep!" Tom yelled. "Get in here!"

A Cylon arm darted through the hatchway, grabbing for him. Zarek grabbed a rifle from the floor and clubbed at the thing until it withdrew. He hit the hatch controls. Other metal arms banged against the door as it sealed closed.

The Cylons had crushed Boone. The Creep had to be dead, didn't he?

He moved to the window. He saw nothing but Cylons, three in a pile where he had last seen the Creep, the rest surrounding the now still form of Doctor Fuest.

Wait! He saw someone else moving, over by one of

120

the Vipers. None of the machines noticed. The Cylons' attention was focused elsewhere.

Somehow, Slam was on his feet out there, climbing back into the cockpit of his Vipes.

Tom jumped back to the wireless. "Vipes Three! This is Zarek! Let's get the hell out of here."

Slam's voice came through a moment later. *"Glad to hear there's somebody else alive. Follow me out, huh? I'll get us back to Lightning."* He made a sound that was half laugh, half cough. *"Then I've got to see the doc."*

Tom looked at the rows of controls before him. He realized he had to fly this thing. Zarek mimicked what he had seen Boone do only hours ago, flipping the twelve switches. He felt the engines come to life beneath his feet. The screen before him showed the Viper launching from the far side of the field. He eased the stick forward, worried he would fall too far behind.

The lander lurched off the ground as the Viper roared into the air.

Something pinged off the lander's shell. The Cylons were firing at him! He doubly wished the Creep was here now, to lay down some return fire.

He'd just have to follow Slam home.

The next few minutes were pure nightmare.

Zarek managed to get the lander in the air, copying Boone's movements as best he could remember. But the squat ship jerked and rolled. He had to right the craft or he'd crash right back down into the landing field.

He grabbed the stick and tugged. The lander righted itself—and it was rising! He could still see the Vipes in the distance, though it was far smaller than the last time he had looked.

But they were free of the base! Now, if he could just stay on the Viper's tail . . .

The stick wouldn't stay in one place. He had trouble keeping the lander flying in a straight line. It dipped again, swooping down toward the planet before he got it heading back aloft.

He looked back to the screen, hoping he could still see Slam's Vipes. He saw something else instead.

Another, bigger ship was showing up on his screen. It blotted out one quarter of the view. That thing had to be close to the size of a Battlestar—maybe even larger. Where the hell had that come from?

He flipped on the wireless. "Vipes Three! Slam! What's going on?"

"Incoming fire! I've got some monster ship on my tail! Trying evasive maneuvers."

The transmission cut off abruptly.

The lander shook. Tom was tossed out of the chair, jamming his shoulder against one of the guns still strapped to the wall. He pulled himself up to look out the window.

In the distance, where the Vipes had been flying, he saw only a ball of flame. And above the flame was some huge, dark object that took up a large part of the sky.

Frak getting back to the *Lightning*, Zarek thought. He was headed straight toward that thing. Whatever had gotten Slam was going to get the lander next. He had to make his tiny ship less of a target.

He crawled back to the controls and cut the engines.

Without a heat signature, maybe the lander would become invisible to the monster ship above.

The lander, not yet free of the planet's gravity, stopped its ascent and began to fall, slowly at first, toward the surface far below.

He looked at the controls. If he could cut in the thrusters at the last minute, maybe he could cushion the landing enough to keep both the ship and himself from getting hurt without giving too much of a signal to his enemy. That was a big maybe. But if he could do it, once the huge ship had disappeared from the sky, he could still find some way to get back to the *Lightning*.

The systems were still working. He needed to open the wireless and let Nadu know what was down here.

He decided he had to risk a short message on the ship's secure frequency.

He flipped the SEND switch, and spoke quickly:

"We were attacked. They have a warship in orbit. I'm the only one who got out, and I can't see a way of getting back to the *Lightning*. Captain, the base was crawling with Cylons!"

He was coming in at an angle. He'd have to wait and use the forward thrusters to cushion his fall. He remembered—vaguely—how Boone had held the stick as he prepared to land.

Zarek hoped he could remember a lot more.

He tried to figure out where the lander would fall. He was some distance from the research station. From his trajectory, he guessed that he had flown south. The screen showed the world beneath him as a mass of green.

The ground was coming up fast. Zarek threw on all

four thrusters beneath the vehicle while pulling back on the stick.

The lander seemed to hesitate for an instant in its descent, then began to turn end over end. Zarek cut the thrusters and let go of the stick. The rolling continued.

He strapped himself into the seat at last. He could no longer tell from his instruments which way was ground and which was sky.

The ground rushed toward him. Zarek hit the thrusters and prayed to his parents' gods.

A jolt ran through him as he heard a horrible rending noise.

Everything went dark.

CHAPTER

11

"What the frak?"

Nadu stared at the monstrosity on the forward screen. It was one of those old supercruisers, built before the war, ten times the size of the *Lightning*. If it was fully operational, it would be fitted with fore and aft cannons, over one hundred Vipers, uncounted missiles and probably a few weapons Nadu no longer remembered.

No way the *Lightning* could stand up to that kind of behemoth. A ship like that could swallow the *Lightning* whole.

"Captain?" different members of the crew called out, reacting to his silence. "Orders? Do we fire?"

A part of him wanted to stay and fight. He had five of his own on the far side of this warship, looking for the two that had gone before. Seven out of a crew of nineteen.

He had never lost this many men.

"Captain!" Griff shouted. "We're getting a radio signal from the lander."

The message was heavy with static. *"We were attacked. They*—static—*warship in orbit. I'm the only one who got out, and I can't*—static—*getting back to the* Lightning. *Captain, the base was crawling with Cylons!"*

"Zarek. That was Zarek," Griff said. He frowned, staring down at his comm controls. "We've lost the signal."

Nadu had known before his lost crewman had used the word. The Colonies had long ago abandoned those old ships, replacing them with Battlestars. The monster in front of them was a Cylon vessel.

His crew had been attacked by Cylons. He'd lost seven of nineteen. With that thing in front of them, he had no way to see if any were still alive.

They had flown into a trap. Nadu had been careless—worse, he had been blind. He had operated in a universe where the Cylons were long gone. A place where you could profit from a terrible war, and pick up the pieces from a time of terrible destruction. Now the Cylons had come back to change the rules.

Seven of nineteen. And what could he do?

"Out of here!" he called abruptly to his crew. "Chart a course, get us as far away from this ship as possible. We can't outgun them. Maybe we can outrun them."

His crew shouted to each other to strap themselves in. Absently, Nadu returned to his chair. He sat as *Lightning*'s engines roared to their full capacity.

They ran from the fight, ran until they could get far

away to safely Jump. The monstrosity on their screens was growing smaller. No one spoke, all waiting for some reaction from the other craft.

Seven of nineteen. And what could he do?

He turned to his dradis man. "Was there any sign of the lander?"

"No, Captain, no sign. None at all. But it was hard to see anything else close by the warship. They were shooting at something—something my instruments picked up. It could have been the lander or a Viper. Then it was gone."

He didn't say what Nadu was thinking. The warship must have shot the lander out of the sky.

The warship was growing ever smaller. The Cylons hadn't fired on them.

"Captain!" the dradis man called. "They are not pursuing. The other ship is moving away!"

"If we leave the planet," Griff surmised, "I guess we're no longer a problem."

To the Cylons, the *Lightning* was insignificant. The fact only increased Nadu's rage.

This was not the end of it. But how to pay back a ship full of Cylons? Nadu welcomed the right sort of death. But not suicide. He had lost seven. He could still save the other twelve.

For half a minute, he thought about going to the authorities. See what that outdated warship might do when confronted by a dozen Battlestars. But he doubted the authorities would even listen. They all knew Nadu's reputation. They would come up with a dozen reasons to arrest him instead.

No, he would not involve the Colonies in any official capacity. But that didn't mean he was done with this.

The Cylons had not seen the last of the *Lightning*.

Nadu hummed. He had an even better idea.

"Captain," the dradis man called, "the warship has disappeared."

"Gone to the far side of the planet, no doubt," Griff added.

Had the warship been hiding all along? The Cylons must be guarding something on the planet. Something really valuable. Nadu's instincts were never wrong.

"Captain! We have reached the Jump coordinates!"

Nadu nodded. "We're out of here—for now."

He stared at the screen as the crew made the final preparations to Jump. "We have to assume no one was left alive." He looked to his second in command. "We go to the safe coordinates. Griff knows the way."

It was Griff's turn to nod. The comm man looked surprised.

Nadu added, "We have to have a little meeting of our own."

Zarek opened his eyes.

He was still strapped into the chair. He looked around the inside of the lander. A few things had shaken loose, but not much. Boone had been good at stashing things away.

He had seen Boone die. And the others. All but the Creep, who had been lost under a pile of Cylons. He was probably dead now, too—or worse.

Tom was the only one left. The only one free. The only one still alive. But for how long?

He tried to move. He was sore, but nothing seemed broken. The chair must have taken most of the impact.

The lander was sitting at an odd angle. He imagined something was damaged. He could hear the hiss of compressed air from somewhere behind him.

He unstrapped himself and pushed away from the chair. He stepped carefully across the slanting deck.

He looked out the window. He was surrounded by trees. And nothing but trees.

Everything was quiet. No one was after him, at least not quite yet. So he had survived.

He hoped the *Lightning* had gotten his message.

He took a slow walk around the tiny room, letting his fingers brush against the walls, the instruments, the secured weapons and supplies. He thought again how good Boone had been at his job. Almost everything was unbroken and in place. The ship itself was damaged, but its contents were more or less unscathed. The cabin appeared to be intact. The primary destruction was probably belowdecks. The hissing sound came from the other side of the storage hatch.

He supposed he should check it out, in case the sound meant something worse. He unlocked the hatch and pulled the door aside. Tom frowned. The cargo area had not fared as well as the cabin. The cases of extra supplies had pulled loose from their ties to jumble together in a great pile. At least one of the containers had broken open, spilling its supplies on top of the rest.

He saw no obvious source for the noise. He might have to pull that whole pile apart to find it.

The hissing stopped abruptly. Tom closed the hatch. For now, he decided to consider that problem solved.

He hoped it was just a broken air line. He no longer needed the air filtration system. The air outside was perfectly breathable—unless he ran into some unknown: insects, pollen, parasites—that might give him trouble. Only one small corner of this world had been claimed by the Colonies. Was the rest of it safe? He would have to open the door and find out.

He supposed it had been too much to expect that he could land this thing unharmed. He was lucky he was still in one piece himself. Without repairs far beyond his ability, this lander was never leaving this exact spot.

But he could stay here for weeks. He could survive most anything. The supplies belowdecks might be jumbled, but they appeared largely intact. He had food, water, air, weapons, even Boone's survival kit. He was set for a while—until what?

Would Nadu risk a rescue against a Cylon battleship? For one lone crewmember? If Nadu had even gotten Zarek's message in the first place. As crazy as the captain was, he always protected his crew. He always bragged about how few he had lost.

The lights in the cabin still worked. Zarek didn't dare try the engines. He wondered what else he could use. He turned to the wireless, slowly spinning the dial, and was rewarded with a loud squawk. He turned the dial back, then tried it a second time. This time he got nothing, not even static. He had lost communication with the outside world.

Maybe he could find some old manuals to read around here. Maybe Tom could even teach himself basic shipboard repair. He had gotten a pretty good look at his surroundings. He decided the next step would be to take an inventory. Boone was so thorough, you'd think he'd leave some sort of documentation behind. Unless the pilot had carried all the manuals in his head.

Without the engines to regenerate their charge, Tom realized, the batteries would run down eventually. He would have to shut down most of the lander's systems in order to preserve some of the batteries' power. If he could keep the batteries charged, and if he could repair the wireless, he might be able to send a second distress call.

Unless that would bring the warship down on his head.

He had too many questions. He wished he hadn't been the only one to survive. He didn't see much hope.

Tom shook his head.

What now?

He didn't know how far from the research station he had landed. It couldn't be too far. He hadn't gotten very high off the ground before he had had to cut his engines.

Part of him wished he were much farther away, somewhere the Cylons couldn't find him. But he had no idea if the machines would even come looking for him.

Maybe landing only a few hours away from the Cylons could work to his advantage. If he couldn't get the lander to work, maybe he could steal another ship. Not that he'd know how to fly it.

If he got desperate enough, he knew he would try anything.

Part of him didn't want to leave the lander. He sat inside the crippled ship for who knew how long, trying to figure out his options. He didn't have many.

He had to learn to live without the ship's comforts. He could continue to use it for shelter, at least until he determined what, if anything, lived in this place.

He knew it was time to pop open the door. He realized that he was pacing around the small cabin, resisting that next step. Staying in the lander was staying with the familiar. Once he opened the hatch, he would be admitting that he was facing the unknown.

But what was he afraid of? He had always wanted to be a figure of authority. So long as he went nowhere near the research station, Tom Zarek was king of the world.

But he couldn't even laugh at his feeble attempt at humor. As far as he knew, all the others in the landing party were dead. He was a survivor. He would have to be resourceful.

He had to pop the hatch and take a look outside. Eventually, he would have to venture a little farther, and find out exactly what he could do with this new world around him.

Tom Zarek would find a way.

He walked across the cabin and hit the hatch release.

Griff was running the show now. Grets said it was about time. Griff smiled at that. As the ship's cook and doctor,

Grets was as close as anyone was in the corrupt crew of this bucket to having a soul.

"So we're heading for—where exactly?" Grets asked.

Griff shook his head. "Nadu only gave me numbers, with nothing to go with them. I memorized these coordinates seven years ago. He never asked me to use them—never even referred to them again—until now."

"So Nadu has another plan? That's not much of a surprise." The lines of her face wrinkled as she smiled. The crew said, between cooking and meds, Doc Grets could make anything right.

"I think the captain will let us know, once we get there," Griff replied.

Not that the captain was much in evidence of late. Nadu had locked himself in the captain's quarters, and would open the door only twice a day, to take food.

"Do you think I should do something?" the doc asked. "He almost always talks to me." In fact, Griff knew, Nadu would talk to Grets before anyone else on the crew.

"I think it's best that we all leave him alone." They'd run into Cylons and lost an entire landing party. This was nothing with a simple cure. "When we get to where we're going, he'll be ready. We were caught by surprise. That won't happen to Nadu twice.

"Wherever this ship is going," Griff added, "I just hope our captain plans to bring the rest of us along."

CHAPTER

12

RESEARCH STATION *OMEGA*

The landing field was very quiet, where a moment before it had been full of weapons fire and the sound of engines.

The companions who were guarding Doctor Fuest stepped back, allowing the doctor to see the daylight overhead.

He stood, and for the first time saw the carnage, both the dead bodies and the shattered companions. Until this moment, the doctor had had no idea such a thing could happen.

Gamma watched him impassively. "It would be best if you returned inside."

Doctor Fuest could find no words. But he couldn't move until he had said something.

"What have you done?"

"Our apologies," Epsilon replied. The companion

dropped its gun to the ground. Now that the threat was over, all of the companions had let go of their weapons, while other domestic models were gathering them up. One white kitchen companion had gathered two dozen rifles in a cart before it.

Fuest hadn't known the research station had so many weapons.

Oh, he was always aware they had had considerable firepower, even though he had never approved. The guns, grenades, and whatever else had been brought when the station was first founded, some years before the war, had been stockpiled to fight a threat that had never come. Before today, he had considered the underground storage facility an unfortunate part of the station's past. He had never even opened the weapons vault since he had become the leader of the center.

The companions obviously knew about both the weapons' uses and deployment. He realized it would have been a part of their original programming. As shiny and new-looking as they were, many of these machines were older than the doctor.

The research station's purpose had always been to add to their original natures, and to find a way for these glorious machines to reach their full potential. Nothing had ever been done to remove their initial programming.

Doctor Fuest now realized that may have been a mistake.

The doctor had gotten some brief glimpses of the carnage despite being covered by his guard. Gamma and Beta, derived from a Cylon Butler and Cylon Mechanic model, had not joined in the fight. But Epsilon had used its weapon as if it were an extension of its arms. But then Epsilon came from the warrior models, an improvement on the old Harbinger of Doom prototypes. He remembered how their original leader, Doctor Jaen, had proudly pointed to these new models, now called Centurions.

Some of the new experimental Centurions had come with built-in weapons systems, systems that Fuest and his team had disabled close to twenty-five years ago. He wondered, absently, how easily the warriors might be refitted with those systems again. At least it hadn't come to that.

The doctor was surprised at the thought. Was he expecting all-out war?

Part of Fuest felt that that was what he had just survived. The companions had surrounded him in such a way that he could only get occasional glimpses of the violence. But he had heard every shot and every scream.

He turned to Gamma. "Why has this happened?"

Gamma bowed forward slightly, its white-enamel exterior glinting in the sun. "We were warned of this type of human."

"They would not have acted in your best interest," Beta added. "We felt it was our duty to protect you."

Fuest frowned at the thought. "How could you know what kind of humans they were?"

"We have researched their craft," Gamma replied. "They have old systems—from before the war—systems designed to interface with Cylon technology. These are parts they found on abandoned outposts, that they have refitted into their own hardware. We can access their codes, and download their records."

Epsilon stepped forward to enter the conversation. "They are unauthorized scavengers—you have another word: pirates. They would have been as likely to kill you as to help you."

Fuest found his shock being replaced by anger. "Who are you to make such judgments? They were the first outsiders we had seen in thirty years! We could have found a common ground."

"We could not take that chance," Epsilon replied. "Not when we saw that they had weapons."

"You yourself have often said how unpredictable humans can be," Gamma reminded him.

He looked from one companion to the next. He found their emotionless visages—which he had often taken to be the peace of the saints—to be infuriating at this moment.

"I have not seen others of my kind in half my lifetime! And before I can even talk to them, you . . ."

The three companions looked to each other, as if silently conferring.

"Humanity is spreading again, leaving the Colonies to search the stars," Gamma said at last. "We will see others."

"Before I'm gone?" the doctor asked. "Unlike you, I have little time remaining."

Gamma paused. "I can assure you that others will arrive shortly."

138

They seemed so certain, they made the doctor hesitate as well.

He took a deep breath and looked out at the late afternoon sky. "Very well. We will convene, at midday tomorrow. We will discuss what happened, why it happened, and make very sure that it will never happen again."

Gamma bowed slightly. "Of course, Doctor, we would never do anything that would disrupt the real purpose of this station."

"We are as dedicated to that as you," Beta added.

"There are so few—humans—left," Epsilon said. "We wanted to protect every one of you. How can the station go on unless both of us are here?"

The doctor nodded at the wisdom of that. "Very well. Tomorrow, I want all the senior staff to gather. I am very shaken by this. We must find a way to go on." He stared at each of the senior companions in turn. Why did he feel that there was something they weren't talking about? He repeated his primary worry: "I want you to assure me that this will never happen again."

The three paused another moment before each spoke in turn.

"We will do our best."

"We will find a way."

"You know, Doctor, that we only want to work together."

The doctor took a deep breath. What they said was true. It had always been true. He realized he was exhausted. "Very well. It would be a shame to lose everything we've done."

"We are all in agreement," Gamma answered.

"Very well. Could you help me back inside? I'm very tired."

He had to rest more and more these days. His life was fading. It felt like he was losing his grip on the station as well.

The three companions gathered around him: the Mechanic in highly polished silver, the Butler all in white enamel, and the Soldier, in a burnished darker tone, near to black. Beta and Gamma stepped closer to lend their support, while Epsilon led the way back toward the door to the station's center.

Sometimes he imagined he could hear emotion in their voices. But their still metal faces betrayed nothing.

He supposed it was an old man's fancy, this giving human emotions to machines. He hadn't really looked at the companions closely in a very long time.

"So you were able to access this new ship's records?" he asked as he slowly walked toward the door. "I didn't realize you had those capabilities."

"It is one of many programming functions that are not often used," Gamma explained. "It came into play as soon as the ship appeared within range."

He wondered what else the companions could do that he had forgotten about. He was sure it was all in the original research. He wished once again that Betti was here. This was much more her area of expertise.

"They would have stolen from you and done you harm," Gamma continued. "Our fundamental programming directives say we must protect you. We could see no other way."

"Theirs were the first guns produced," Epsilon said from where it walked ahead. "We only protected you."

"We will remove all evidence this occurred," Beta added.

Fuest was tired. It could not be undone. He allowed them to lead him back inside. They were efficient machines. But, as machines, they could see none of the ramifications of their actions.

The senior staff would have to sort this all out. He would assign the children to check the companions' programming, to find ways to prevent this from ever happening again.

If the companions were correct—and they had never lied to him—there would be other visitors. He hoped they were both more official and more trustworthy.

Next time, Research Station *Omega* must be truly prepared.

Laea had seen it fall.

She was hoping that this meeting would be a new beginning. She would have no more of the little world she had grown up in, full of men and machines that told her what she could and couldn't do. She would meet other people—people who would lead her to new and different places. It was a brand-new world.

Her brand-new world had been torn apart.

She could not believe what had happened. Before today, her mechanical brethren had never shown the faintest signs of aggression. Ancient programming must have overtaken the companions.

When the shooting began, the companions blocked the doors, not allowing any of the humans to watch what was happening down on the field. No doubt the machines would claim they were protecting the humans.

But Laea wanted no more protection.

She didn't stay with the others. Her brothers stared in horror at the landing field. Ten times worse than the last time, they said. They, too, told her not to look.

Nobody watched her leave. They only wanted to keep her safe. She walked away from the death, away from the noise. She was safe, she knew, so long as she was behind closed doors.

But she had never planned to stay inside. Once away from the field, she was questioned by no one. She saw no one. She felt as if she were the only one inside the entire station.

She easily got up onto the roof, and carefully crawled over it toward the field, worried that some stray bullet might come too close, but too curious and excited to stop herself.

The gunfire seemed to die down after a while. She peered over the edge and saw a body lying on the ground, close by one of the Vipers. She gasped. Half the pilot's face had been blown away. This was the first time she had ever seen a human in a pool of blood. Parts of companions were littered around the body, and something wet—lubricant from the machines, perhaps, or fuel from the Viper—had started to burn.

It was terrible, but she couldn't stop looking.

She realized why the station had seemed so empty. It seemed like every companion on the base was out on the field. She had forgotten how many of the machines were here—close to a hundred, she guessed. And most of them were now carrying weapons.

Someone shouted below. Two of the ships were taking off. The Viper Mark One rose in a graceful arc. The other seemed to barely get off the ground, then jerked farther aloft to follow the Viper.

The companions all turned to look at their escaping foes. A few shot at the slower craft, but both ships seemed to get away safely.

Her gaze rose to follow their trajectory. This time, she actually cried out.

She saw a new ship in the distance. It was a large vessel, unlike any she'd seen in her research. Its appearance was similar to some warships she had seen, only far more massive. She guessed the ship hung miles overhead, yet it seemed close to the size of the planet's smaller moon. She supposed that was an illusion. No ship could be that large.

The Viper, only a dot now with a bright trail of fire, flew up and above the oncoming craft, reaching for the sky.

Suddenly, a single jet of flame came from the large ship. The Viper exploded in midair.

The other ship, still far closer to the surface than the Viper, paused abruptly, as though it had lost its engines. It dropped like a rock toward the forest below.

The large ship hung in the sky for a moment, as motionless as that newly discovered moon, then slowly moved away.

It was suddenly very quiet.

Laea realized that she was probably the only human to have seen it all.

She saw how the companions clustered around the doctor, protecting him from harm, perhaps, but also keeping him from seeing the true nature of the damage.

They guided him back inside the hangar.

The remaining Viper was wheeled away out of sight. She wondered if she would ever have a chance to look at it.

She knelt on the edge of the roof as all the parts left behind of men and machines were scrupulously scrubbed away.

It took very little time at all.

She decided it was best to climb down from here, to reenter the station before anyone realized exactly what she had seen. She would go back to her room, tell everyone that the noise had been too much for her to handle. Wide eyed, she would ask the others to describe what had happened.

She wondered exactly what their answers would be.

They had killed the humans so quickly. And where had that great ship come from? Could it be another vessel from the Colonies? But why would they shoot down a Viper?

The companions suddenly seemed so unlike those gentle machines that helped to raise her. After this, she wasn't really sure she knew the companions at all.

But what would happen now?

The companions were the doctor's whole life. Man and machine working together—it was his life's work. He wouldn't change his mind no matter what happened.

The research station was a small place, and everyone shared everything. Or so Laea had thought.

She had never seen a reason for secrets. The companions heard everything. And the companions shared many things of interest with their four human counterparts.

The companions had become so much a part of their lives, they were almost invisible. She and her brothers treated many of them like friends. Sometimes they forgot they were there, almost like furniture.

But the companions also spoke among themselves, exchanged data in ways far too fast for humans to even comprehend. Laea had found ways to listen in to many of these exchanges. Most were about technical data, having to do with the station's ongoing research. But there had been a few messages she could not understand, messages with symbols and number sequences she had never seen before.

She still hoped there was a logical reason behind all of this. But they all seemed very different than they had a few hours before.

How could she look into the true heart of a machine?

She wanted to talk with Jon and Vin about what she had seen. But she knew that could only happen if the three of them were alone.

They might have to leave the station to make that possible.

She had to have an honest talk with her brothers. Alone. She would tell them what she had seen, and see if they could tell her anything about the giant ship in the sky.

Maybe the fallen ship would give her some answers. She would very quietly get the station's systems to find it. And then she would take a look at it for herself. She needed simple, straightforward answers.

Somehow she knew she would get none of that from the companions.

CHAPTER

13

BATTLESTAR *GALACTICA*

"Enter!"

Admiral Sing looked up as Captain Draken, the officer of the watch, stepped through the doorway into the admiral's quarters.

"Thank you for seeing me, sir. I thought it was important that I show this to you in private."

"Yes, Captain. So you said on your wireless call." The call had sounded very urgent. Now, Draken looked uncomfortable, as if he would rather be anyplace but here. "And what is this exactly?"

Draken held out a small disc. "It's a distress call, sir." He glanced down at the recorded message. "More specifically, it's a wireless communication we picked up a few hours ago. We think it may have something to do with the ship we found. It was encoded, but it was a very old code, and simple to break. The signal was pretty faint, but we managed to boost it enough so you can make out the words."

The admiral nodded to a small slot on his phone. "Why don't we play it here. And you think it's from the scavengers?"

"I've probably said too much, sir. I think you should hear this for yourself."

Sing nodded and waved the other officer forward. He had never seen the young man so distracted.

"We worked on this overnight," Draken explained as he inserted the disc. "The duty staff in the CIC all heard it before I could get a really clear idea of what it was." He coughed. "I wanted to bring it to your attention before it got all over the ship."

The disc played its very short message. With the last words, Sing understood Draken's concern.

Cylons.

Something like this would spread like wildfire. "Very well. I think we should have a meeting of all senior staff." He checked his watch. "At oh-eight-hundred hours."

"Very good, sir."

"And I want to meet in the CIC. I'd like as many to hear this as possible, before the rumors get too far."

"We were attacked. They have a warship in orbit. I'm the only one who got out, and I can't see a way of getting back to the *Lightning*. Captain, the base was crawling with Cylons!"

Adama knew now why Sing had brought the dozen members of the senior staff here to hear this—besides Adama, the circle included the ship's doctor and chief engineer, the Viper captain and the men and women that ran the other important functions on board. Each one could tell their subordinates exactly what they had heard here, and what they had subsequently discussed and decided. And they were playing the message right in the middle of the CIC—where everyone could hear it and the subsequent discussion by the senior staff. There were no secrets here. It would be the best way to quash the rumors that were no doubt already circulating around the station.

"You all heard that?" Sing asked. Everyone nodded.

"And this message came from where?" Bill Adama asked.

"Captain Draken?" Sing asked in turn.

"We've determined the signal came from somewhere around here." Draken pointed at the star charts displayed on a large screen before them. "We're quite close. Probably the only reason we picked it up at all."

Tigh grunted in disbelief. "There's nothing there!"

"Star charts have been wrong before," Adama reminded him. "We're dealing with information supplied by the individual Colonies, information that dates back to before the war."

Tigh frowned at the thought. "So we may have come across something that some government doesn't want us to see?"

"Exactly."

"Or there may be nothing there," Sing cautioned. "This could be nothing more than a wild goose chase."

"Or a trap?" Tigh suggested. "Maybe the scavengers are looking for some slightly used Vipers?"

The admiral considered the suggestion. "That seems particularly unwise. These raiders have the reputation for being ruthless, and anybody who chooses to make his living out here may be a little crazy. But they have to know that the fleet would send a Battlestar. The scavengers haven't survived so long by going up against far superior odds."

"Maybe it's something set up to scare others away?" Draken suggested.

Adama nodded. "What's more frightening than Cylons?"

No one had an answer for that.

"So what next?" Sing asked. "Recommendations?"

"We have to take this message seriously," Adama offered.

"We go in and take a look," the ship's engineer chimed in.

"We should send out a Viper squad—maybe three planes with experienced pilots? I'll lead them in," Tigh volunteered. "It's not like I haven't seen Cylons before."

"I agree," Sing replied. "We have to treat this as a serious threat. Let's get the *Galactica* a little closer before we send in our team. In case you do get something on your tail, we want to be able to blast it out of the sky."

He paused as he looked at his officers. "But you realize this may be nothing at all.

"Tell all your subordinates. Tell them about this, but call it what it is—a message of unknown origin. We're going to investigate this message, but that is all we know. While it could be Cylons, the possibility is still remote. I will inform Fleet HQ of our decision, and keep them up to date with our findings. If we do find something, we'll have every Battlestar on this side of the Colonies here in a matter of days."

He paused again before he added, "I don't want anyone to panic. This could have any number of explanations. Or it could be somebody's idea of a cosmic joke. Understood?"

The senior staff once again murmured their assent. He didn't want any alarms sounding among the troops. Word of mouth could turn a single Cylon into an entire fleet overnight.

"Remember," he added, "we are no longer at war. We signed an armistice two decades ago. No one has seen a Cylon in years!"

"And I hope we don't see any either," the ship's doctor chimed in. It brought a laugh from all around.

"Maybe," said the admiral thoughtfully, "if we do meet them—we can open negotiations. Maybe we can keep from ever having another war."

Adama was impressed. The admiral knew just what he was doing, ending on this. He reminded them all that the Cylons weren't unbeatable. The Colonies had fought them to a standstill once. Maybe neither side was eager to resume that battle.

"Good," Sing continued. "Then go back and talk to

your people now. Let them know they need to be ready. But don't believe anything until we see it for ourselves. Dismissed!"

The crowd began to leave.

"Captain Adama," Sing added, "you have the CIC. Plot a course for that empty corner of space. If you need me, I'll be in my quarters." The admiral followed the others from the room.

Saul stayed behind. He walked up next to Adama and took a look at the star chart.

"Just like old times, huh, Bill?"

Adama smiled. "Let's hope not. The war is one place I don't want to revisit, ever."

"But we know something about the Cylons. There may just be a reason they've put veterans back on board."

"Well, let's hope we don't have to gain too much more experience." He slapped his old friend on the shoulder. "I am glad you volunteered to lead the exploratory team."

Tigh shrugged. "I couldn't see who else could do it. Oh, I've got a couple of good youngsters who I think would do all right, but most of them are green kids. This exploration stuff I have them on is nothing more than a glorified training mission."

"We were all green once," Adama reminded him. "We were tested, and we came through."

"At least we lived to talk about it," Tigh agreed.

Bill nodded. "Let's hope your pilots don't have to become too tested too quickly."

Tigh's gaze focused somewhere far past the star

charts. "With Cylons, you can never tell much of anything." He glanced back at Bill. "They shot down a few too many of my friends. I never felt like I was quite even. Part of me would like to finish the job." He looked back at the charts.

"How long until we get there?"

"I'm guessing a day, maybe two," Adama replied. "I'll let you know as soon as I finish my calculations."

Tigh nodded. "I'll go and tell my kids. I think some of them would like a challenge. But let's hope the challenge comes up empty."

CHAPTER

14

THE WILDERNESS
OUTSIDE RESEARCH STATION *OMEGA*

Tom Zarek had nothing but time.

By late morning on his second day, he knew his surroundings pretty well.

He was in a valley. Fruit grew on trees, and a small stream passed only a few hundred steps from his front door. He could hear the call of something in the trees. Small birds maybe. So he was surrounded by some sort of wildlife. The birdcalls made the place seem a little less threatening. It was a nice surprise.

Tom's next surprise came when he opened the survival kit. Not only were all thirty-three items inside clearly labeled, but the kit actually came with instructions, with separate entries for each item.

He saw things he could use immediately. And other things—first aid and the like—that he could use over time.

He inspected the outside of the lander, which appeared to have crashed down through a group of trees. That might have lessened the impact of his fall, but it also brought a lot of branches down with it. That caused substantial damage to one corner of the ship, tearing a hole the size of his fist in the outer hull. He imagined some seal had been broken as well—that was probably the hissing he had heard. At least he told himself that. Without any guides to the structure of the lander, he really knew nothing.

The only thing he knew was that the lander wasn't going anywhere, anytime soon.

It had gotten dark a couple hours after his crash, and Tom had made himself as comfortable as possible in the copilot's chair. He slept fitfully, waiting, he guessed, for some large beast to pull open the hatch, which he had left closed but unsealed. But he had heard nothing. He had wondered then if this place had any animal life at all.

In the morning, he had taken his first exploratory walk, a few hundred paces toward the rising sun, then, after returning to the lander, a few hundred paces the other way. It was on his second trip that he had found the small running stream.

At midday, he had returned to the stream and taken water samples, which he tested with Boone's survival kit.

Tom didn't think anything had ever had a truer name. The kit gave him something to read, and instructions that told him what to do without making a frakking

fool of himself. He wished that Boone had left more instructions elsewhere.

Everything else was going to have to be trial and er-
ror. He followed the instructions, mixing the water with
a small packet of powder—the book said the results
might take a couple of minutes.

Tom Zarek had nothing but time.

Now that he was away from the *Lightning*, he thought
about it more than ever. He was a raider. They were all
raiders. Before he shipped out, Tom hadn't really known
enough about what he was to become.

It was a strange crew. A bunch of outcasts, thrown
away by society. Nineteen loners, all tossed in together.
Many were people he might have avoided in his old life.
Most were not too different from Tom Zarek.

In one way, he fit right in. In other ways, he worried
he had made the worst decision of his life.

There were all sorts of stories about raiders. The best
made them out to be clever businessmen, working just
outside the law. There was a lot of money to be made and
no one got hurt.

That was the polite version.

He had also heard stories of raiders gone wild—
scavengers as thieves and murderers, as bad as the bar-
barian hordes of ancient history. Men with no rules who
took what they wanted and destroyed anything that got
in their way.

After shipping out on the *Lightning*, Tom believed
there was some truth to both stories.

Not that it mattered anymore. Once you shipped out

with a raider, there was no going back. You were there for the duration.

Most of all, he thought about the stories he had heard, about the *Lightning*, and about Nadu. "Pragmatic" was a word used for a lot of raiders, but for Nadu in particular.

It wasn't until he was deep in space that he started hearing the most brutal of those tales, and he realized it was a short step from pragmatic to ruthless.

Symm and Twitch had liked to tell the most horrific yarns. Like the one about a planet where those abandoned by the war had reverted to barbarism. According to the story, Nadu had killed those that resisted, and left the rest of them to starve. Or the story about the Colony where all the men had died of disease, leaving only the women behind.

These stories were almost like tall tales, the sort of thing that happened long ago when Nadu first captained a ship, told by one crewmember to another as they passed the time between missions. Tom supposed it really didn't matter whether the stories were true or not. It was the message behind the tales—when you were on the *Lightning*, you would do anything ordered by Nadu.

The Vipe pilots used to roar with laughter if you showed the slightest distaste at their tales. Now, he supposed Symm and Twitch could laugh in their graves.

The crew was an odd mix. Some, like Symm and Twitch, he could see as killers. Others, like Boone and Grets, seemed more like survivors, hard-edged people who were down on their luck.

You couldn't stand on the sidelines. According to their late Viper pilots, Nadu forced you to make a choice.

Tom had hoped it wouldn't come to that. He needed the money. But he didn't want the rest of it on his conscience.

It was one thing he didn't have to worry about now.

The water had turned milky, then clear again. According to the survival manual, that meant it was safe to drink. The manual listed other tests he could perform on the local flora and fauna. He might try those eventually, but for now he would stay with the plentiful rations Boone had brought on the ship.

Zarek looked down at the small cup of water in his hands. Safe water, no immediate danger, no wireless, no immediate hope of escape.

That just about covered it.

He was the only survivor of a massacre. He could say he had survived worse, but this time it would be a lie.

He just needed the Zarek luck to hold on until someone came to rescue him . . . if someone ever came.

CHAPTER
15

BATTLESTAR *GALACTICA*

They were sending the Vipers to explore a world full of Cylons. Captain Tigh had mixed feelings about all this. He walked quickly to the flight deck, where both Viper pilots and deck crew were waiting.

He would do a good job. They would all do a good job. Many back home thought this mission—this exploration of the edges—was going to be easy. Sure, they might find some leftover mining sites where equipment had grown dangerously fragile with age, or have to fire across the bow of a couple of raiders to keep those scum off their tail. But mostly, he knew the fleet sent them out there to train someplace safe and far away from Colonial politics, a place where all the green recruits could learn their way around a Viper, just in case they were ever needed if things came to a head between a couple of the worlds back home.

That might have been one of the reasons Bill convinced the higher-ups to hire Saul Tigh. This was supposed to be light duty. Ease him into the job and see how he handled it, find out whether he was ready for some real work in the fleet.

He stepped out onto the deck, and Athena called the crew to attention. Tigh snapped off a salute as he continued to approach. Twenty-four pilots and close to a dozen flight crew returned his salute.

Well, the real work had shown up, right here, right now, out on the edge of frakking nowhere. And he had to take his green recruits straight into what might be one hell of a battle.

Tigh knew it could be worse. All of them knew their way around a Viper by now. But only four of his two dozen pilots had any substantial flying under their belts, and only two of those showed a real aptitude for battle.

Well, he guessed that made it easy for him to choose who was going to go along on this little mission. He just hoped this assignment didn't explode into something much bigger. His green recruits would have to gain a lot of experience in a hurry.

He stopped some twenty paces away from his assembled troops. Everyone waited expectantly, at attention, for what he had to say. "At ease!" he called. They all relaxed, but only a bit. It was best to get this over with.

"Well, this is it, boys and girls," he called out in a loud voice. "The big time. Just like back in the war, we're going out there to face the unknown. As Viper pilots, we are always the first line of defense. We are fast and deadly. We get in there, take a look around, and hop back out before anybody even knows we've been there."

A few of the pilots laughed. They were trying to release the tension. He knew just how they felt.

"Of course," he continued as he walked down the line, looking straight at each of the pilots in turn, "it all depends on just what we find down there when we go sightseeing. I've decided to lead the first squad down, just three Vipers to take the first look-see."

He could already see relief on some of the younger faces, knowing their crew leader was going to take responsibility.

"I'm asking two of our more experienced pilots to join me. Athena—" He nodded to where the young woman stood at the far end of the group. "—and Skeeter." He waved to the skinny fellow standing in the middle of the newbies. "You will follow me in and watch my tail. As for the rest of you, I want Squads One and Three to be ready for deployment at a second's notice. We may need you to lay down protective fire, just like we did in last month's war games. If we run into trouble out there, I want you guys to make sure we all get back alive. Is that understood?"

"Yes sir!" came the ragged reply.

"Good. We will be leaving in a matter of hours. I will give you the exact time of the mission as soon as it is given to me. Until then, get some rest. Dismissed!"

Most of the pilots quickly left the flight deck. Only Skeeter and Chief Murta, who was in charge of making sure every one of the Vipers would be ready, stayed behind.

"Sir!" The gangly youngster hurried toward Tigh.

Saul paused. "Yeah, Skeeter?"

"Is it true that they've got Cylons down there?"

Tigh nodded. "That's what I hear. We won't know, though, until we see them for ourselves."

It looked like the young man wanted to say something else. Tigh wished he'd just come out with it.

"Is there a problem?" he asked at last.

"No, I guess not, sir," Skeeter replied. "I guess I just thought I'd never see this day."

Tigh smiled at that. "I think a lot of us thought that. You have to remember. We are no longer at war with the Cylons." That was something he should have said to everyone. He would have to correct that oversight before they began their mission. He paused, then added, "But I would not trust those damned toasters for a minute.

"Now, if you'll excuse me, I've got to go play some cards."

Skeeter turned and jogged off to meet the others. The kid was always on the move. Tigh hoped he could use some of those lightning-fast reflexes when they came up against some trouble.

But the talk had gone well. Tigh admitted it. He talked a good fight. He would be all right in the clinch. His experience would see him through. It was the waiting that got to him. He couldn't sleep when it got this close to the action. He had to find other ways to relax.

Now what should he do until the mission?

He would go down to the mess and unwind. A little

light gambling with the troops. And he would allow himself one stiff drink—just one—to take off the edge.

"We're going on our first real mission," he said in the barest of whispers, "and you're not going to frak this up."

He took a deep breath. Once he got going, he'd be fine.

Adama looked at the picture again. His other life. His two sons and his wife, smiling on a sunny day. A part of him was always with his family. He had talked about moving back to Caprica for good.

And then he came to explore the edge of space.

The *Galactica* might have found the Cylons all over again.

Adama realized a part of him looked forward to the danger, the same part that felt truly alive only when there were battles to be won.

He felt alert and ready. And oddly calm.

This was the sort of thing the *Galactica* had been sent here for. This was what he was made for.

He didn't know if he could give this up, even for the sake of his family.

He hoped his wife could understand. She should be proud of him defending the Colonies. But could he be proud of himself, when he felt he was running away from his family?

Adama thought about the old man. Admiral Sing was the picture of calm, no matter what happened around him. He was an anchor, and he kept his whole crew steady around him. If Bill Adama ever got a command of his own, he hoped he could manage it half as well as the admiral.

Now, one way or another, they were going to investigate that distress call. When they grew close enough, they would attempt to hail the planet by wireless. Hopefully, they would get some response, and they could make a peaceful landing. If not, the Vipers would go in on full alert.

He knew Tigh sometimes doubted himself. It would be good for him to see some action. His old friend's heart had always been in the right place, even when he doubted it himself. That's why Adama had recommended Tigh for the job. When things were tough, he didn't know anyone whom he trusted more.

"*Bill.*" Sing's voice on the comm brought Adama out of his thoughts. "*Could you come up to the CIC?*"

"Be right there, sir."

It was time for all of them to see some action.

"We're getting close to the coordinates," Draken explained as soon as Adama joined the junior officer and Sing at the Command Center. "And, as should probably come as no surprise, there is indeed a system ahead, with one habitable planet."

"So this is our mystery planet?" Adama asked.

"Well, it's certainly a place of some interest," Sing replied. "We seem to have tripped some sensor. Mark? Could you turn that up for us?"

A brittle-sounding voice boomed over the speakers: *"Warning! Do not approach! We are under quarantine! Disobeying this command will result in serious consequences! Per order of the Colonial Science Protectorate! Warning! Do not approach! We are under quarantine—"*

"Mark?" Sing asked again, making a slicing motion with his index finger.

The comm officer cut the feed.

"Some sort of recording," Sing added. "It repeats on an endless loop. I imagine this was designed to scare wanderers away—raiders, freebooters, opportunists. It certainly doesn't apply to us.

"As far as they know, we are the Colonial Science Protectorate. We'll soon take care of this." Sing turned to the wireless operator.

"Send a message back. Inform them that, as a ship in the Colonial fleet, we are duly appointed representatives of the Colonies. We are here to call an end to the quarantine." He grinned at Adama.

"Do you think that will work?"

"We can hope, can't we?" Adama replied. "Maybe they'll call us right back and invite us down."

"Sir!" The comm officer passed Sing a message pad.

"Give me a minute," the admiral said. He quickly looked over the text. "This clears up some mystery."

He looked back at those around him.

"We know more about them now," Sing explained. "I've gotten a message back from the fleet. This planet did host a research station before the war, a station sponsored by Picon. Picon! I remember how the politicians from that place would act up before the war. They were always such a pain in the—" Sing hesitated, and took a look around the room. "Anyone here come from Picon? Well, that problem was years ago. Colonies kept secrets from each other back in those days. That bled into the war. First between the Colonies, then with the Cylons. A lot of the secrets got lost. Like this one down here."

Sing looked back at the pad, quickly scrolling down through the notes.

"They lost touch with the station. The Colonies assumed it had been destroyed long ago. Especially considering the nature of their research."

"And that would be?" Adama prompted.

"Cylons," Sing looked back up at his XO. "Just a few years before the war, they shipped out a few dozen scientists and a few dozen Cylons—the latest models, some of them quite experimental, from what I understand. Some bright souls back on Picon felt the relationship between man and machine wasn't working to its full potential. They came here to form a more equal human/Cylon relationship."

Adama considered this. His thoughts surprised him. "That idea would have had merit, back then," he replied slowly. "Handled properly, it could have had real results. Had more people thought that way, we might have prevented a war."

"If that is indeed what the Cylons wanted—to be equal to humans," Sing reminded him. "Even after the armistice, you know, we never knew what really started it all. Still, it's possible. This station has been down there, and apparently fully functional, for thirty years. With luck, we'll see the results of the experiment." Sing shook his head.

"When we go down there, how do you propose we handle the Cylons?" Adama asked.

"It's amazing this place still exists. Who knows how close it is to its original goals?" Sing replied. "In this place both humans and Cylons have been cut off from both sides since early in the war. We may have no problems with the machines down there."

"Or—" Adama prompted.

"They are still Cylons, and we have learned not to trust them. I don't think our lessons will be turned around in a day. Do you?"

"No sir."

"You're going to be our personal representative down there."

"Me, sir?"

Sing nodded.

"You've always seemed able to stay one step ahead of situations around here, thinking about what's going to happen next. I still notice these things even though I'm an old man."

The admiral sighed. "This whole assignment was supposed to be a walk in the park, you know. They needed to give me one more trip before I retired. Me being a war hero and all, it couldn't be behind a desk. So they gave me this. I don't want to be remembered for some battle from twenty-five years ago that I mostly just managed to survive. This backwater exploration trip is my final chance at glory. Maybe we'll get a little bit of it, despite what they thought back at Fleet HQ."

"We're getting a response sir!" the comm officer called.

"Put it over the speakers," Sing ordered.

"Yes sir!"

"*Galactica, this is Research Station* Omega. *Please respond.*"

"This is *Galactica*. This is Admiral Sing, commander of the *Galactica*. It's good to hear that you're still there. We understand you've been out of touch."

"*I am Doctor Fuest, the acting head of the station. We didn't even know if anyone knew we were still functioning! We're glad to hear the sound of your voices,* Galactica."

Adama and Sing glanced at each other. They sounded friendly enough down there.

"Research Station *Omega*," Sing continued. "We are coming down to see you. We have accessed the old Colonial records. We know you have Cylons there."

"*Well, yes,*" the voice on the wireless replied, "*We don't call them that. We try to have a different relationship with our intelligent brethren. We call them companions.*"

"You know that we haven't seen a Cylon in over twenty years?" Sing asked.

The doctor hesitated before he replied. "*I didn't. I knew of the beginning of the Cylon-human war. But after all this time, I thought you would have found a way to make peace.*"

"We did, after a fashion, twenty years ago. We had an

armistice then. But the only way we could find peace was a total separation of man and machine."

"I am sorry to hear that. I guess we have done things differently here than the way they are done elsewhere in the Colonies. I believe each of us has something of value for the other."

Adama thought, *Now wouldn't that be nice? Perhaps, if the universe was a different place.*

But then, in this small corner of space, it was a different place.

"We look forward to your visit." The doctor paused. *"We have had earlier visitors, with unfortunate consequences."*

Another pause.

"Please bring no weapons, and we will bring none either," the doctor said at last. *"We have had a very unfortunate event happen recently. We were visited by a group of I believe they call themselves raiders. It did not go well."*

"Can you explain?" Sing asked.

"People were killed. Companions were damaged beyond repair.

"We do not wish to repeat our errors. We are both a part of the Colonies, even though we have been separated for close to thirty years.

"Will you comply?" the doctor asked.

"We will honor your request," the admiral replied after a short pause of his own.

"Thank you," the doctor replied. *"We very much want to talk in a peaceful fashion. Omega Station out."*

Adama turned to Sing. "What do you think, sir?"

"I'm inclined to believe they are telling some version of the truth. I imagine they need our help. As self-sufficient as they may have been they may need supplies. They may even want to shut down the whole operation, and get back home." The admiral allowed himself the slightest of smiles.

"I imagine we're almost as much of a surprise to them as they are to us."

He clapped Adama on the shoulder.

"I'm going to send you down, Bill, to negotiate. Keep your eyes open—especially the ones in the back of your head."

Skeeter wanted to jump out of his skin. Tigh had called them back together one more time.

The Cylons will get you.

"We have made final arrangements with the Research Station," Tigh was saying. "The plans have changed. We will accompany the shuttle, but we will not land. As long as those on the station keep their part of the bargain, we will as well."

If you don't finish your dinner . . .

Skeeter never thought he would actually see a Cylon. Maybe now he didn't have to.

He was a trained pilot. He would only see them from high in the air.

In an odd way, he felt disappointed.

If you don't clean your room . . .

Maybe, if he could see them for real, he wouldn't

need to be scared of them anymore. Maybe he could banish the old woman's voice once and for all.

"We are an escort," Tigh continued, "and will keep a watchful distance. The remaining Vipers in the Commander Air Group will remain on full alert until further notice. We will be flying out with the shuttle in thirty minutes. That is all."

So Skeeter was still flying, just not as far.

Why couldn't he shake this creepy feeling?

The Cylons will get you.

CHAPTER

16

RESEARCH STATION *OMEGA*

Until today, Vin had thought his job was the easiest of all.

The three "youngsters," as the doctor called them, despite the fact that they had all passed twenty, all had separate jobs at the research station. Laea took care of the farming and other outside duties, while Jon functioned as the doctor's assistant, an increasingly important task as Doctor Fuest slowed with age.

Vin worked with the companions. He had been fascinated with them since he was small.

It had started with the accident that had taken out a whole building of the facility, and claimed all their parents' lives. At first, Vin had blamed the companions for his parents' deaths. They were efficient machines. Why hadn't they been able to detect the overheating coils and fuel leak that had caused the explosion? Had they wanted the humans to die?

But over time, Vin had seen that a far greater number of companions had perished in the blast. And he had come to view the remaining companions as hardworking and knowledgeable, each within its own designated area of expertise. But any one of the machines by themselves was far from all-knowing.

He had learned the quirks of the companions over time, how Gamma worried about the doctor's health while Epsilon constantly watched the station perimeter for any signs of change. Even though they had learned new tasks at the station, each companion was still true in part to its original manufacture. He had learned to repair and maintain each and every one of them, and had even helped Beta in the design of newer models.

He could talk to the companions. He wished he could talk to humans as well. Jon was so caught up with his aid of the doctor, he rarely seemed to have time for anyone.

And Laea . . .

Laea had become a woman, a beautiful young woman. The three of them—Jon, Vin, and Laea—had grown up as brothers and sister, and had treated each other as such.

Until now.

Vin could hardly stop thinking about her.

She was his sister. You didn't think that way about your sister!

But she was the only woman he knew.

He did his best not to stare at her. He found it uncomfortable to be alone with her, uncomfortable to talk when she was in the room.

So they kept their distance.

But now the outside world had come, and the companions were showing signs of ancient programming that even they had seemed to have forgotten. They were surrounded by violence that he had never seen from the companions before.

He thought he knew these machines very well. Did he?

Maybe Vin needed to take a step away. Maybe he needed to reconnect with the other humans, to make that extra effort to talk to them as the people he remembered from childhood.

The station was changing around him faster than he could understand. But parts of change could be good.

Jon, Laea, Vin. Perhaps they would all start talking again.

But could they talk enough to save the station?

Laea stared at the table in front of her. She had rarely found a meeting so pointless.

They sat in their usual places around the long table. The companions were on one side, the humans on the other. She wondered why they always sat this way. She had always assumed it was the doctor's wish, or the wish of whoever had come before the doctor. But their positions separated them, establishing an order that seemed to contradict the mandate of this station. It had not been so bad before, at those hundreds of other gatherings she had taken part in over the years. Back then the doctor would take time to compliment some new initiative of the companions', or Vin would make some of his lame jokes about the station breaking down. When they were young, Laea remembered how amused she had been when Beta would extend all its wrenches in the air and twirl them all at once. They had felt more like a family then. Now, it seemed they had no joy, no pleasure left in their lives.

It all seemed very odd. No one was pleased with what had happened. At least they had determined that much. No one knew what to do. But everyone was willing to go on with the meeting as if it might accomplish something.

Only a few moments ago, she had thought this meeting was going to tell them everything. Why the companions had anticipated violence. What had happened to the Viper. Who or what controlled the great ship in the sky. But she only heard the same words over and over.

"We were unaware of the problem," Gamma said for maybe the fourth time. "It will not happen again. We will make the proper adjustments throughout the companions."

"We are here as equals," Epsilon spoke up at last. "Is that not the case?"

The doctor stared at the companion.

"That was our purpose here," he answered at last, "the reason this station was created. We all know that. But our protocols insist that you defer to the station staff in a time of emergency."

"Doctor," Gamma replied, "we have been in a time of emergency ever since the second accident. Since that event, the companions have learned to perform every function on this base. We do not want to lose you. As you have seen by our recent actions, we will do everything possible to protect you. But, if and when you can no longer function, the base will go on."

The doctor was silent. He nodded his head once.

Beta took up the argument next. "We only want what is best for all of us at the station. Perhaps we acted rashly. But you insisted on being in the open, a potential target. The scavengers thought you had taken their first pilots prisoner. We surmised that they might want to take you prisoner and force an exchange."

The doctor blinked as if just now remembering something important. "Did you take the pilots prisoner? You said something about that before."

"Are they alive then?" Jon broke in. "Why haven't we seen them?"

"We have been busy preparing for other contingencies," Epsilon replied. "They are well taken care of. We knew you would want to see them eventually."

"But you have not brought this matter—the prisoners—to us," Jon countered. "We are supposed to work as a team. It seems that you are taking on a great deal of the responsibility yourselves."

"We have been taking on responsibility for day-to-day routines for quite some time," Gamma added. "It was natural for us to take responsibility for crisis management."

"We need to be able to manage all functions of the research center," Epsilon joined in. "As you yourself have stated, Doctor, you will not be with us forever."

Laea knew what was different. The three companions spoke almost as one, as though they all shared the same ideas. Before, they had each seemed a bit closer to the nature of their individual manufacture. Butler Gamma was all for efficient station operation. Mechanic Beta worried about keeping everyone and everything operational. Warrior Epsilon was concerned with procuring foodstuffs—birds and fish mostly—for the humans—as well as bringing up points on defense, which, until recently, they had never seemed to need. Now the companions seemed to be finishing each other's sentences.

She noticed something else as well. The companions had always used a deferential tone with the doctor, the legacy, she guessed, of their original Cylon programming. Now they seemed to challenge him. The current crisis had brought out something new in the companions.

Maybe that was the difference she had noticed over the past few days. It was the purpose of this research center to see if both humans and machines could benefit from a newly structured society. In the early years, Laea understood, they had thrived. As long as she could remember, they had had to depend on each other to survive. But the founding humans had always taken the lead. Now, perhaps it would be better if the more capable companions would take control.

No one disputed the companions' remarks. Instead, Jon discussed how to make plans for any similar events that might happen in the future. She realized that Vin hadn't spoken at all. She found him glancing moodily in her direction a couple of times. Did he feel the same way she did?

Laea found her attention starting to wander. This morning, using her personal computer, she had plotted the likely trajectory of the fallen ship. She had hoped there might be taped records of the landing, but the stationwide system marked them as "unavailable." She had frowned when she first read the word. Did that mean no records had been kept during the chaos around the scavengers' arrival? Or were other members of the senior staff reserving them for study?

She worked out the final coordinates without the help of the machines. For some reason, she felt the need to keep this very much to herself. She definitely saw some changes in the companions of late.

If they could keep secrets, so could she.

She had already thought of a number of reasons for her to leave the compound. Some of the farming area needed to be upgraded. They required some new soil to properly grow the vegetables. She would tell the senior staff she needed to spend the day taking samples. That is, if anybody bothered to ask.

She seldom left the research center. None of them did anymore. Years ago, she and her brothers used to explore. They used to do everything together.

What she did was every bit as important as what anybody else did. She could fix most anything. The companions brought her those things not covered in their programming. Sometimes she and the companions repaired them together.

No one had time to talk to her now. But why?

"Is there anything that anyone would like to add?" the doctor asked. His traditional ending to every meeting.

No one spoke, and the meeting ended. As she left the meeting, she realized she hadn't spoken either. Why didn't she tell the others about the ship?

It was her one true secret.

Her one moment of freedom—away from all of those who didn't care . . .

Now that the meeting was over, she would find out what had happened to the small ship—and she would do it for herself.

Tom Zarek would walk a little farther every time than he had before, and he would walk three times a day. Now, two days in, he had a good idea of his surroundings.

He took a knife and marked trails around his new home. He memorized the quickest way to the stream, and found that it led down to a slow-moving river. He had even found a small cave—small and empty, he was pleased to discover. It would give him another place to go in case the lander was discovered.

He slowly climbed out of the valley, in the direction that his lander had flown and fallen. When he climbed to the top of the ridge and stood in the clearing between the trees, he could see a distant shine, tiny glints of silver in the distance. He was quite sure that glow was the top of the towers at the research station.

It made him realize how close he really was, how little

altitude his lander had gained before it plummeted back to the planet's surface. He guessed the station would be less than a day's walk from here, even with the uneven terrain.

That also meant that, if the Cylons were coming for him, they would have been here by now. He doubted that Cylons would have to do anything as primitive as walking.

That thought made him feel just a little bit safer.

His exploration nearly done, he did his best to patch up the comm system. He found a small set of tools in a compartment beneath the pilot's seat, and decided it was time to look at the innards of the wireless array.

The front panel came off easily. He grabbed the high-powered light he had found in the survival kit and shined it inside. It was something of a mess.

The crash had jumbled some of the hardware, pushing whatever had sat above the wireless into the wires below. A couple of those wires had pulled free, while another, which seemed quite long, had torn apart in the middle. Any or all of them could be what ailed the wireless.

Two of the wires could be reattached, but the third one was a total loss. He hoped he could find some other similar wiring elsewhere in the ship.

He looked for other panels that might be easily opened in other corners of the cabin. He found five, all full of various circuits and a few very short wires. Nothing was quite as long as the missing wire, though he saw some that he thought he might splice together.

When too tired to walk or mess with the ship's innards, Tom took inventory. He had forty-eight different types of guns on board. Maybe Boone had been more frightened of what was going to happen than Zarek had thought. Most of the weapons he knew. A couple were so large he found them a bit intimidating.

And though the variety wasn't great—most of it was surplus rations packed to last for the long term—Tom figured he had enough food for the better part of a year. Supplemented by the safe local drinking water, and—perhaps eventually—some experiments with the local vegetation, and maybe a bird or two, Zarek could last out here indefinitely.

He had enough food for months. He had enough firepower to last a lifetime.

But to what end?

There were times when he just sat.

He had water. He had food. He had his thoughts.

Tom Zarek had a bit too much time to himself.

He wondered why he was the only one to survive.

He went over the whole sequence of events. Although it had seemed to take a very long time, he was sure the battle had not taken more than a couple of minutes.

He saw himself walking ahead to greet the welcoming committee.

He wondered if Ajay had even gotten the message on his faulty equipment. Or had he seen something from on top of his Vipe? He saw the white Butler model cut off Zarek from the old man. Were the Cylons already planning to attack?

He had no way to know.

The whole thing was rather ironic.

Of all those from *Lightning*, he was probably the

worst fighter in the bunch. He had been in a few street brawls when he was down on his luck, but nothing with guns or grenades or even knives. The others had been with Nadu longer, and from their stories had seen all sorts of action. Boone was the type of guy who seemed able to do anything. And the Creep—well, Zarek imagined he'd killed quite a few.

Tom realized he was alive because he was the only one not brandishing a gun. His role as peacemaker, and his proximity to the old man, had saved him.

But one Vipe pilot got shot through the head, the other blown out of the sky. Boone died with a final blast of defiance, and gave Zarek a chance to jump into the lander. He still wished he knew what had happened to the Creep. Before this, Tom had thought that guy could have slipped free of anything.

It was far too still out here. He heard the wind and a strange whooping sound in the distance. He guessed it was a native bird. At least there was something else alive! But he listened for other sounds, he listened for voices. Was he waiting for the Cylons? For rescue?

Sometimes, he felt as though the others who died would come to haunt him.

He thought he heard a noise, then, out in the trees. Was it the Cylons at last? He didn't breathe for a long minute. Nothing followed. Maybe the local wildlife was getting a little closer.

He shifted his position—he was sitting by the lander—and listened again. He heard nothing but that odd and distant bird noise. If something had been rustling around in the underbrush, it had probably been scared away.

He needed to get out of his head and back to work. He looked at the lander. If he couldn't get at any useful wires from the inside, maybe he could get something out here. The crash landing had given him a ready-made hole. He stuck his fingers in the ragged space, then pulled his hand free—the edges were sharp. He pulled off his shirt and wrapped it around his hand, then carefully placed his cloth-wrapped fingers back in the hole. He gave the piece of metal a tentative tug. The whole thing came away from the ship with hardly any effort. And it revealed a gift from the gods—a mass of wires, all far longer than he needed.

Tom quickly stepped inside the ship to fetch the tool kit. The right wire could get the comm system up and running. He could listen for his rescuers, maybe even send out a distress call. And what if the Cylons picked it up? If he was stuck out here long enough, Zarek realized, he wouldn't care who got it, as long as he got out of the wild.

Many of the wires seemed to branch off some sort of junction box, just below the edge of the torn metal hull. If he could just pry one of them loose. He took a small rod with a sharp edge from the tool kit, and poked it toward the junction. It slipped past the wires and cut into some soft membrane. A dark, heavy liquid squirted along Tom's arm and into his face.

He cried out, leaping out of the way as the liquid arced briefly out of its new opening. It stopped after only a few seconds, but the damage had been done.

Frak it all! Tom used his shirt to wipe the stinging liquid out of his eyes. It itched where it had made contact with his skin. He realized he had better wash it off as quickly as possible. He dropped the tools on the ground and headed for the stream.

This is what he got for trying to be a mechanic. He jogged quickly to the water and plunged his arm into the cool, flowing stream. To his relief, whatever the viscous fluid was, it came off easily, leaving only the slightest of red marks behind. He dunked his head in the water to clean off his face, then threw his shirt into the water, too, to see if the water would clean off the stuff that had gotten rubbed in. This was his only shirt. If he lost this, all he had left was an atmosphere suit.

He lifted the shirt from the water to take a closer look. The dark stain had turned a dull gray. Maybe if he scraped it on some rocks.

He stopped looking at the shirt when he saw the other face staring at him. It was a face between the trees, on the far side of the stream; the face of a young woman.

His mouth opened. There were other humans here? He stood up quickly.

"Hey!" he called.

The face had disappeared.

"Hey! Who are you? Don't run away!"

He heard crashing in the bushes, and then nothing. Not even the strange calls of the local birds.

CHAPTER
17

Adama landed by himself, and without incident, on the empty landing field.

"Welcome to Research Station Omega," the now familiar voice announced over the wireless. *"We will come out to meet you."*

Adama stepped out of the shuttle. He saw the doors open wide on the side of a building at the far end of the field. Three men stepped through the door and walked toward Adama's shuttle. They were followed by three Cylons a moment later.

Adama opened the shuttle door and stepped outside.

As the six others walked toward him across the field, Adama noticed that one of the men kept glancing behind himself at his metal companions. They were close enough now so that Adama could recognize the three different Cylon model types. Adama had fought the Warriors, and had run across a few of the Mechanics. He didn't think he had seen a Butler model since before the war.

The party hesitated maybe fifty paces away.

Adama supposed there would be tension at their first meeting, but this seemed particularly awkward.

He took a few quick steps away from the shuttle and toward the other party. He was careful to keep a good amount of room between them.

He saluted the assemblage, human and Cylon, and spoke in a voice loud enough to cover the distance between them.

"Colonel William Adama, of the Colonial fleet."

All six of them bowed slightly in return. Adama wondered if this was some anarchic custom from the Picon High Court. It certainly looked exceedingly formal.

The three humans were all male, one quite old, the others much younger. The elderly man at the center of the group spoke first.

"I am very, very glad to see you." He waved to those around him. "All of us are glad to see you. I am Doctor Villem Fuest."

He turned to the three Cylons behind them. "May I introduce you to Gamma, Beta, and Epsilon. Three of our companions." He pointed to the Butler model, the Mechanic, and the Warrior in turn. Seeing them this close, Adama realized the models were slightly different from those he remembered from his younger days, when Cylons and humans shared the same worlds.

These are not the same Cylons I have fought. He would have to remind himself of that as long as he was here.

Adama realized he was expected to say something. "You'll have to forgive me. This is the first time I have seen Cylons in over twenty years."

The doctor shook his head. "They are Cylon in design, perhaps. But our companions are a new breed of being. We have tried to change our way of thinking here. And we have had a great deal of success."

"I'm eager to hear about it," Adama replied. "My people are eager to hear your whole story."

The doctor glanced at the young men to his left and right. "Oh. But I haven't introduced Jon and Vin." Adama guessed the younger men would be in their early twenties, close in age to the Viper pilot recruits back on *Galactica*.

"But as to this project," the doctor continued. "Whatever happens, I would want this center to go on. With the proper supplies, perhaps we can still invent the perfect society."

Many things were possible. But after all that had happened in the war, could Cylons and humans ever work together? Adama would do his best to reserve judgment.

"But what do you want from us?" the doctor asked.

Adama had rehearsed this answer on his way down to the planet. "First and foremost to reestablish contact. We have been sent by the Colonies to explore all those outlying regions once settled by humanity, to claim them again as our own. They're curious at home to see exactly what is still out here."

The Cylon Butler—Gamma was its name—stepped forward and spoke briefly with the doctor.

Fuest looked back to Adama.

"I'm afraid some of us are not quite so trusting of your intentions. The companions already see problems."

"We did as you asked," Adama replied. "I came down, alone and unarmed, the executive officer, second in command on the *Galactica*. I think that should be symbol enough of our good intentions."

Gamma spoke directly to Adama. "We know about your Viper escort."

Adama replied directly to the Cylon. "We made promises as to who would come down here. We made no promises as to who would be in the air. So, yes, we have Vipers on alert." He paused before asking, "And you are without contingency plans?"

The Warrior Epsilon stepped forward. "Our weapons are stored where we can obtain them quickly."

That statement made one of the young men—the same one, Jon, who had turned back to the Cylons—look rather uncomfortable. Adama resolved to talk to Jon at his first opportunity.

The doctor turned to the Cylons. "This isn't like before. This is civilization. These people come from the Colonies that created this station."

"Would you like me to send the Vipers away?" Adama asked. "We can have more of our people come down shortly, after we talk more about what we both need."

The doctor smiled and shook his head. "No, no, why

not have them come down and join us now? That way, neither side will look as though they are threatening the other. We will welcome them as well as you."

Adama was a bit surprised by that response. He did his best not to show it. "Either way, I'll have to send a message from my shuttle." Adama pointed at the small ship behind him.

"Why don't you do so?" the doctor agreed. "I'm glad, this time, that neither of us has had to jump to conclusions." He shook his head. "We had earlier visitors, quite recently. It did not go well." The doctor looked down at his hands, then back at Adama. "I'll tell you about them when you are done with your call. Most unfortunate."

"We saw signs of raiders in the area," Adama replied. "Is that who you are talking about?"

"Yes, raiders," Epsilon agreed. "We sent them away."

"Perhaps we could take you on a quick tour," the doctor said a bit too brightly. "If you want, I'll certainly let you look at our records. We've done great things here. I would hate to see them end."

"Well, we're certainly willing to help out however we can," Adama said. "We are a fully stocked ship. Our supplies are at your disposal."

The smile fell from the doctor's face. "What do the Colonies want? What will you do with us?"

"We have no orders concerning you. Until a few hours ago, we didn't even know you existed. What would you like to receive from us?"

The doctor thought a moment before replying.

"I think I would like to see Picon again. As to the youngsters, I guess you would have to ask them."

"How many youngsters are there?" Adama asked.

"One more besides Jon and Vin. Our human population is not what it once was."

That led to the next obvious question. "And how many Cylons?"

"Our companions?" The doctor turned to Gamma. "Close to one hundred."

"Ninety-seven," Gamma spoke up. "Four of that number are currently undergoing repair."

"After the accidents. Companions could be rebuilt. Humans could not." The doctor smiled apologetically. "I would hope we could have new scientists come out here and continue our work at close to the old levels of staff. We were so close to success before the accidents."

"Let me make a call," Adama said, waving back at the shuttle, "and then I'll be ready for that tour."

"Most certainly," the doctor agreed. The rest of his party, both human and Cylon, stood silent.

Adama returned to his ship. This meeting was awkward, but it did not seem threatening. His first impression was to trust this odd mix of man and machine—for now. If they were truly open about their records, the Galactica might even be able to discover important data concerning the Cylons—data that could help them get ready for the next time humans and Cylons met.

He settled into the pilot's chair and clicked on the wireless.

"Shuttle One to *Galactica*. I need to talk to the admiral."

"He's been waiting for your call," the voice on the other end replied. *"I'll put you through."*

"Colonel Adama," Sing's voice answered an instant later.

"Admiral Sing," he replied.

"Good to hear from you, Bill. What's your status down there?"

"Our initial meeting went well. They seem friendly enough, and I believe they are sincere. But it's also obvious that they haven't had visitors in a very long time. They are aware of the Viper escort circling overhead. And they aren't particularly happy about it. They asked if the three Viper pilots would like to join me, and I told them I'd do my best to get them down here. Frankly, I could do with some friendly company."

"So you think there's nothing more to the research base than what we were sent by Picon? It's just an old Colonial project that managed to survive?"

"That's my first impression. They seem to be opening up to us to a point. But this human-Cylon interaction is very strange. It's throwing off my judgment in everything. That's the best reason for the Viper pilots to join me. I could use a few more sets of eyes."

"Very good, Bill. I'll order the three Vipers to come on down with you. And I'll ready Plan Beta, in case you get into any trouble."

"Copy that, Admiral. Adama out."

Plan Beta would put twice as many Vipers in the air at the first sign of trouble. Bringing the first three Vipers down was a gesture of peace, but that gesture had an iron fist hidden just behind it. But it shouldn't come as a surprise to anyone on this station that a Battlestar would be prepared to respond to any aggressive act.

Adama wondered if Fuest would even think of such a thing. Maybe it was being cut off from society for so long, but the elderly doctor seemed strangely innocent, as though he couldn't imagine one side striking against the other. From Gamma's actions out in the field, Adama guessed that these new Cylons were fully capable of fighting the Colonial fleet.

Adama realized he was all too ready to return the favor. He hoped it got no worse than simple mistrust.

He rose from his seat and exited the shuttle once more, ready to get a look at the rest of *Omega* Station.

"Viper One."

Tigh was surprised to hear the admiral's voice.

"This is Viper One," he replied.

"Colonel Adama needs a little help. He wants you to come down and join him."

"Is he in trouble?"

"Negative. Everything's peaceful. Let's just say he's unsure if there are any hidden situations. He just wants a couple extra pairs of eyes to take a look around. So you three are going to go down and join him."

Wouldn't that make all four of them much more vulnerable? "Are you sure about that?"

"Sure enough to be making this order personally. Go down, take a look, and report back to the Battlestar. And no weapons. We don't shoot at them until they shoot first. Understood?"

"Understood, sir."

"Good. Bill trusts you on this, and so do I. Remember, you're going down to look at a Picon Colony Science Station. But you'll let me know when you find something else. Sing out."

"Copy that." Tigh didn't have a good feeling about this. But they were going down. Admiral's orders.

He opened the comm link to the other pilots. "Athena? Skeeter? You're with me. Colonel Adama needs us down on the planet."

"We'll follow you down," Athena's voice replied.

"But the Cylons, sir—" Skeeter began.

Tigh cut him off. "Colonel Adama knows what he's doing. We'll land in close formation. Just stick close to me."

"Should we take any defensive measures, sir?" Skeeter asked.

"Definitely not," Tigh replied. "If Adama's down there asking for us, he's determined that the Cylons are not an immediate threat. The admiral personally told me that, when we leave our Vipers, we will do so unarmed. Is that understood?"

"If you say so, sir," Skeeter said without conviction.

"I say so, so let's go. Delta formation." That would keep the other two Vipers just behind and to either side of his lead.

Tigh hoped his own feelings were wrong. He would trust Adama above just about anybody.

But he didn't want to just hand over three Vipers to the Cylons.

CHAPTER
18

She ran.

Why hadn't Laea spoken to the stranger? She had been almost as startled seeing him that close as he was to see her. He was the first man she had ever really glimpsed, up close, outside of her immediate family.

Maybe the lack of a shirt surprised her more. He had stood there, his chest bare, looking tired and lost in the middle of the woods. She hadn't seen her brothers without some part of their clothes since the three of them had been ten. Everyone was always fully dressed. It was the way it was done on Picon, and they carried over those traditions here. She could hear the doctor say those words as she thought them. He always said there was a proper way to do everything.

Laea was also startled by how young the stranger had looked, surely only a few years older than herself. A part of her had always thought that spacefarers would have to have the age and wisdom of the doctor. That was her image of people with knowledge. But this stranger was not much more than a boy, close in age to her brothers.

Without his shirt, she could see all the muscles on his stomach and his chest. She had found herself staring at the man when he looked back at her. She couldn't breathe. She felt as if she had done something terribly wrong. She felt she had to get away.

She had started for home before the man could do more than call out.

Now she wondered why she had come here in the first place. It had taken her three hours, following the river, to reach that spot from the station. She had brought one of the monitoring devices—a sort of heat sensor—that the companions used when they went out hunting for food. She hadn't been sure it would work. The companions usually went in search of large flocks of birds, while she was looking for signs of a single human.

But the monitor had steered her in the right direction. Any closer and she would have blundered right into the stranger . . . the man.

She ran back the way she had come, feeling very foolish. She had so much wanted to get free of everything in the station! She had wanted to find out what had happened to the lander, and what those in the station weren't telling her.

But she had made no real plans, and she realized she had no idea what she wanted to do next.

Maybe she should stop running.

Maybe she should go back and find this man and talk

to him. She could apologize for their meeting, ask him what it was like, outside the tiny world of the research station.

Or maybe this man—this raider—this scavenger—was every bit as bad as the doctor and the companions said, and she was in danger just looking at him.

She knew now she was headed back toward the station. It was her home. It was the best place to be.

This was her first real look at the unknown. She had to get away from that new place, that new man, until she could figure out what to say, what to ask.

Maybe next time she shouldn't come out here alone. What if the young man was really dangerous?

Could she get one of her brothers to join her? These days, neither Jon nor Vin seemed to have much time to talk to her about anything, much less march hours away from the station.

She hadn't really thought out any of the consequences before she had started out here. Now she would be gone for the better part of a day. She wondered if she would have to explain herself. Whether those back at the station even cared.

She heard a roaring overhead.

She looked up in the sky and saw another ship fly above her, a ship not much bigger than a Viper, but more boxlike in structure, like it was designed to carry lots of people and supplies.

Someone else must have found them—unless this was another ship from the raiders. Someone at the research facility must have known about this before she left.

She realized she had been so intent on finding the lander, she hadn't cared what was happening at the station.

She was still some distance from the station. At least she was far from harm if anyone started using weapons again. She hoped nothing else unfortunate would happen this time. She wished there were some way she could stop anything like that from happening—ever again.

But whatever was happening, she had to see it for herself.

Laea climbed to her secret spot on top of the roof, just as she saw three Vipers streak down from the sky. When she reached the spot where she could look over the edge, she saw that all three Vipers had landed midfield. These three were newer models, more streamlined and shinier than the ones the scavengers had used. She watched as all three pilots climbed from their ships. They were all dressed in flight suits. Two men and a woman? And Jon had come out by himself to greet them, with a group of companions watching from near the hangar doors.

She would like to go somewhere where a woman could fly.

Jon stopped in front of the three pilots. Everyone seemed happy to see each other. This was different.

She realized she was missing out again on the life of the station. She wanted to meet the new people, especially a woman who flew a Viper.

She guessed, for that, she would go down and join them.

* * *

Tigh stepped out of his Viper.

"Holy frak," he said.

This looked like something from his childhood. Cylons and humans, side by side. His family hadn't been rich enough to have Cylon servants, but he had seen them everywhere.

The first time he had been up close and personal with Cylons it was a few years later, and he was trying to kill them before they killed him. Now, looking at the half dozen machines clustered at the far side of the field, he realized he had this built-in fight-or-flight pattern he would have to overcome.

He had thought getting back on the *Galactica* would be a good test of whether he had a future. Until this moment, Tigh hadn't realized how much he would be tested.

An actual human being walked between the Cylons, heading toward them across the field. Athena smiled as he approached. She seemed relaxed despite the things that waited for them on the far side of the field. Tigh would never understand that woman.

Not that he didn't find her attractive. Tigh always liked a take-charge woman, and Athena certainly fit that description. But it wasn't good practice to fraternize with those under your command. Tigh had screwed up in so many ways over the years, he didn't want to do the same thing here.

Maybe Athena was just too young to remember much about the Cylon War. But then Skeeter looked worse than Tigh felt. From the frown on his face to the way he jumped at the slightest movement around him, the young pilot seemed to want to be anyplace but here.

"I never thought I'd see these things, sir."

"Well, they're not supposed to be the Cylons that we fought," Tigh replied, realizing he meant his words to reassure himself as much as Skeeter. "They have some sort of experimental program here. Cylons and humans get along."

"If you say so, sir."

Tigh nodded. "I have trouble believing it myself." He waved at the young man walking toward them. "Let's go meet the fellow. Until we're told otherwise, everybody and everything here is our friend. Is that understood?"

"Yes, sir."

"Athena?"

She fell into step beside the other two pilots. The young man slowed his own forward progress as they approached.

"My name is Jon," he called out to them. "Your Colonel Adama is looking around our center. I've been sent to bring you inside so we can all join him." He turned abruptly, calling over his shoulder, "Follow me!"

He was leading them straight back toward the cluster of Cylons. Without any weapons, Tigh was feeling increasingly naked with every step.

Jon waved at the machines as they approached. "As you see, we live in harmony with the companions."

"That's what you call them?" Athena asked.

"We call them that, because that's what they are.

This place only works because we all—human and companion—work together."

Jon led them back through a large set of doors. A half dozen Cylons watched them pass. All of the machines were built to look vaguely human, with a head-shaped object above what could be a pair of shoulders. But their faces were all curiously blank and unformed, often not much more than a few blinking lights. Tigh saw models with long broom arms that had once been used for street cleaning, a multi-armed mechanism of the kind that he remembered had cooked for large groups, and a couple of the silver mechanical repair models with dozens of interchangeable parts. He had almost forgotten how many different varieties of the machines had once existed, before the war had turned them all into killers.

"We developed this station to be a self-sufficient community," Jon continued as they entered a long hallway with doors to either side. "Despite our problems, this is no doubt why we survived."

A moment later he added, "If you look to our left, you will see the companion repair facility."

A vast room stretched off to their left. A dozen or more Cylons were working on parts of other Cylons. The bustle of activity reminded Tigh in an odd way of a nest of insects, something compact and contained one minute, swarming all over you the next.

The Cylons inside all paused and looked at the newcomers.

"Up ahead here," Jon called from where he had already walked on down the hall, "we have our main data center, where we are still collecting information from experiments started thirty years ago."

Tigh and the others hurried down the hall to join him. This new door was on their right.

Five different-model Cylons checked vast banks of equipment far beyond Tigh's understanding. They all stopped abruptly, and stared at the newcomers.

"You'll have to forgive the companions' curiosity," Jon said as he once again walked away. "You're the first new humans they've seen in over twenty years."

Curiosity? Is that what he called it? Seeing the Cylon's blank faces staring at them, Tigh thought their reaction could be anything. Hatred, fear, that startled moment just before the enemy attacks. Anything.

They passed other doors, and other Cylons. Each of the "companions" stopped whatever it was doing to look at them as they passed. While this might have been called a Colonial research center, it felt far more like an enemy camp.

"Your Colonel Adama is meeting in our conference center, just through here."

Jon led them through a door, where two humans and three Cylons were seated around a long table. These Cylons glanced briefly at the newcomers but did not stare. After what they had just walked through, Tigh realized their gesture seemed almost friendly.

Adama stood as they entered the room.

Tigh didn't think he had ever been so glad to see his old friend.

Adama saluted them all. "Captain, lieutenants."

Tigh, and the others behind him, all snapped to attention. "Colonel Adama, sir!"

"Everyone at ease. This is Doctor Fuest." Adama waved at an elderly gentleman who sat to his right. "He's been showing me the place." Bill grinned at the doctor. "It's quite impressive. I was about to ask the doctor what results have come of their research."

"We do manage with what we've got," the doctor replied. "The planet provides us with raw materials for manufacture, as well as foodstuffs for the human members of the community. We survive. But we have not grown in the ways we had wished." He paused, then added, "We have the whole history of the station on file. I'm sure that can help you if you want to look for anything specific."

Tigh noticed that the doctor wasn't quite answering Bill's questions. Bill no doubt noticed that as well. He couldn't wait to talk to his friend alone.

"Doctor?" a Butler Cylon spoke up.

"This is Gamma," the doctor said with a grin. "I suppose we should all introduce ourselves again! Yes, Gamma?"

"Laea has returned," the Butler replied.

A moment after he spoke, a young woman entered the room. She was dressed in the same shapeless white tunic and pants as the other humans, though hers were covered with a few stains and wrinkles, as if they had seen some real use.

She stopped and stared at all of them, and then

smiled. "So you are from the Colonies?" She laughed, resting a hand on Adama's shoulder. "It's these uniforms that give you away. I'm glad you're here at last. The doctor's been waiting for you forever."

She smiled at each of the pilots in turn, looking straight at each of them, totally unafraid.

Tigh had never seen a girl quite so at ease, so natural.

"Laea keeps her own schedule," Jon said with a frown. "Although you would think she would make an exception for visitors."

"I am here now, Jon," she said brightly. She smiled at each of the newcomers in turn. "I oversee the soil collection for our farming, and I was out—nobody told me to expect—well, I'm here now, aren't I?"

Jon and the other young man continued to scowl, while the doctor smiled rather benignly. Apparently, young Laea was the problem child around the station. Tigh thought she was charming.

The doctor waved at the four in uniform. "As you guessed, these are all representatives of the Colonial fleet. Our home worlds have found us!"

"But others found you first," Adama replied. "You promised to discuss this."

"We're still not certain exactly what happened," the doctor answered. "Things happened very quickly. The companions acted to protect us."

"It went very badly," Jon broke in. "People died. Companions were damaged almost beyond repair. But after that they left us alone."

"And our mistake with them meant we wouldn't make a mistake with you," Gamma added.

"In what way?" Adama asked.

"You understand, they were the first new humans we had seen in years—" the doctor began.

"These are not scavengers," the Warrior Cylon said. "The protocols are different."

"What looked like an attack apparently activated certain obsolete programs," Jon explained.

"These have been corrected," Gamma added.

Tigh was impressed. Whatever the frak they were talking about, the humans and Cylons did speak on equal terms. Adama didn't act surprised, so neither would he. For now, Tigh thought it best to stand silently and listen.

"Now, your pilots here," Laea interrupted, "what are your names?"

Tigh and the others introduced themselves. Laea quickly managed to introduce everyone else in the room, including the Cylons.

"Would you care to join us, Laea?" The doctor pointed to a chair at his side.

She paused and frowned for an instant before her smile reappeared.

"Would you mind if I showed some of the guests around?"

"I've already shown them most of the points of—" Jon began angrily.

Laea waved away Jon's objection with a single flick of

her hand. "What did you show them? The repair room?
The science labs? We live in a truly beautiful and exciting
corner of this planet. Let me take some of our new
friends up to see the lookout ridge, or our new agricul-
tural stations!"

The two young men looked like they wanted to shoot
her on the spot.

The doctor was far more accommodating. "No, I'd
like them to know as much about the station as possible.
We will have to make some informed decisions very
soon." He turned to their chief officer.

"Colonel Adama?"

"I can discuss the important issues here," Bill said after a moment's hesitation. "I think I'd like Captain Tigh
to stay as well. His experience with Cylon culture might
prove invaluable. But we do want to see as much of this
facility as possible. I think it would be a wonderful idea if
your young woman—Laea?—would show my two lieutenants around."

Tigh's experience with Cylon culture? Like that he
had killed over a hundred of those frakking monstrosi-
ties? Bill was giving him a danger signal, a code that
there was something wrong in paradise.

"Lieutenant Tanada," Adama said to Athena. "Be prepared to give a full report. We really need to learn as
much as we can about this station in a very short time."

"That's wonderful!" Laea said to the room. She
waved to the two pilots. "I'll give you the full tour. The
others will be sorry they stayed behind!"

"Laea!" the doctor called out. "Gamma and I have

decided we would like to honor our guests with a formal dinner. Can you see to it that you are back here by nightfall?"

Tigh was sorry to see her go. She smiled at him as she left the room. He chided himself for his thoughts. There was a considerable age difference. He would have to put young women out of his mind and get down to work.

Adama waited for the three to leave the room before he turned back to the others.

"Doctor. Companions." He looked at the three humans and three Cylons in turn. "I'm afraid we are through with being polite here. As a representative of the Colonial fleet, I outrank anyone on this station.

"Before I can make any kind of final report, you must tell me exactly what happened to the scavengers."

Now Saul saw why he was here. Bill wanted Tigh to back him up in a fight. This was just like old times.

"I will report," the Warrior Cylon Epsilon interrupted. "The cruiser *Lightning* entered our system two days before you arrived. They demanded that we let them land. We had nothing we could do to keep them from landing. This demand also put all the companions in defensive mode. In a way, we were being invaded. We prepared for a violent attack."

"But I asked you to do no such thing!" the doctor protested.

"We sometimes question your judgment, Doctor," Epsilon replied. "We have done it quietly, so as not to upset you."

The Cylon turned its attention back to Adama.

"Two men came down initially. They waved guns and fired upon the companions, even though we held no weapons. We overwhelmed them with sheer numbers, and took them prisoner. They severely damaged three of our number."

"Prisoners?" Adama asked with a trace of anger. "You said nothing of taking prisoners."

The doctor shook his head. "I have not seen them. I meant to, but with all that has transpired . . ."

"I've seen them." Vin spoke up for the first time. "They are in the medical unit, in induced comas. We had no other place to store them. Both pilots have suffered injuries, but I believe both will survive."

"Why didn't you tell me this?" the doctor asked.

"Doctor, you seemed overwhelmed," Gamma replied.

"It was all that death." The doctor whispered one more word. It sounded like "bet."

"The scavengers demanded the return of their pilots," Gamma continued. "We would gladly have given them up, if they had acted in a civilized manner. Five came down the second time. I believe the lead negotiator wanted to find a way to make an exchange. But others in their party were all too quick to draw their weapons. The doctor had gone to meet them. He was in harm's way."

"We had to defend the best interests of the station," Epsilon explained.

"It was over very quickly," Jon spoke up. "Three of the five were shot. The other two escaped in their ships."

"We are not sure what happened to those vessels,"

Beta the Mechanic said. "Our dradis system was disrupted at that time. We feared it had been damaged by weapons fire, but shortly thereafter, it once again became operational."

"By the time we could once again check," Jon added, "the cruiser *Lightning* was leaving our system."

"We were left with prisoners that we didn't know what to do with," Epsilon added.

Adama stood abruptly. "I would like to see the prisoners—now."

The doctor, grim-faced, stood as well. "Very well. Shall we all go?"

CHAPTER
19

Laea wanted to trust them. They came from the Colonies, didn't they—her human home?

She felt she needed to trust someone outside the station. Her home had always had its secrets, but they had grown much larger very quickly. There were things right in front of them not talked about.

The others said they regretted the deaths of the scavengers, but it seemed as if not even the doctor felt for the dead.

And no one spoke of the other ship. The ship she had seen from the roof.

Laea needed to tell them her story.

"I'm glad we got away from the others," she said to the two young pilots. "I need to talk to you, someplace private."

"What?" The young man called Skeeter looked confused. "I thought you were taking us on a tour."

"Oh, I'll be taking you on a tour." She looked around her. "We can't talk here. Everything in this place is recorded for future study."

Athena frowned. "Then they're watching us? Won't they be suspicious if we leave?"

"The station isn't that organized. So much is recorded, sometimes no one bothers to look at what has been saved unless they have a specific reason to. But I have questions, and I'm sure you have questions, too." She smiled up at one of the hidden recorders. "But really, I'm simply showing you our farming sites. It's what I do, remember?"

She led them back out onto the landing field.

"Actually, I need to take you some distance away from the station. It's a bit of a walk. We may not be home for dinner."

"You aren't afraid that someone will get suspicious?" Athena asked.

"No, they'll just get angry," she said with a grin. "I'm known to be irresponsible."

Skeeter looked out at the ships sitting on the field. "You say this thing you want to show us is some distance away? Who says we have to walk?" He glanced over at Athena. "Haven't you flown the shuttle a few times?"

"You don't think the colonel would mind?" Laea asked.

"I think the Colonel wants to find those secrets more than you. What a good idea, Skeeter!" Athena smiled at Laea. "Would you like to take a little trip?"

Laea stared at the squat craft before them. "Could we? I've never ever been in the air."

216

She could fly, just like this woman from another world.

But she had important things to do. This would give her the perfect opportunity to talk with them about the stranger. Maybe they could even bring the stranger back with them.

She looked around the field. "I had better tell someone we're doing this."

Skeeter followed her gaze. "You mean, you've got to check in with *these* things?"

Laea waved away his objections. "They mostly let me do what I want. Anyone will do. The companions all talk to each other." She pointed and yelled across the field.

"Delta!"

A squat, pale beige companion with a padded midsection rolled in their direction.

"Laea!" the companion replied in a high voice. "It has been long since we've talked! What can I do for my little one?"

"Will there be a problem taking off without the doctor's permission?" Athena asked as Delta approached.

Laea shrugged. "He's in a meeting. He told me to give you a tour. And that tour will be from the air. I don't see a problem."

"I'd just as soon take that tour," Skeeter agreed. "I can't get used to these companions of yours."

Delta rolled to a stop before them. "Laea? What have you been up to?"

"Would you tell the doctor that we are going to take the shuttle up for a look around? We won't be going very far."

The companion hesitated for a moment before replying. "This has been cleared with the doctor?"

"Yes, he just sent me to show these newcomers around."

Delta paused before remarking, "I understand you are all expected for dinner."

"And we will be there. Thank you, Delta, for reminding us."

"You're welcome, Laea. Now be a good girl."

It turned and rolled slowly away.

"That Cylon seemed to be scolding you," Skeeter said.

Laea smiled at that. "The companion is a Nanny Model. Quite gentle, really. She was one of those who raised me and my brothers. I think she has trouble talking to me in any other way." She waved to the two pilots. "Now let's get up in that shuttle before Delta talks to anyone else."

Skeeter opened the hatch, and the three quickly climbed inside. The place was full of switches and dials. It reminded Laea of a miniature science center.

Athena sat dead center in front of the controls, and waved for Laea to take the seat on her left.

"I need to talk to someone, too." She flicked a couple of switches in front of her. "*Galactica*, this is Athena."

"Galactica *here*," a man's voice said from a speaker overhead.

"We're going to take the shuttle up a few hundred feet and take a look around the research station," Athena continued. "We've got someone with us who's going to give us a guided tour."

"*Okay, Athena. Is Colonel Adama with you?*"

"Negative. Just Skeeter and me and one guest on this trip. The colonel is currently talking to the head of the center."

"Very good. Please let Adama know the admiral would like to speak to him at his first opportunity."

"Will do, *Galactica*." She flicked a couple more switches. "Well, now we've all gotten permission from everybody."

Skeeter sat down in the next chair over. "You'll need to strap yourself in there. Like this."

Laea copied Skeeter's actions. The belt closed with a satisfying click.

"I need to do a couple things to get us started." Athena glanced over at her as she flicked a series of switches. "So what's life like on the station?"

Laea shrugged.

"Nothing ever really changes. It just goes on. I think it made more sense when there were many humans to interact with the Cylons."

"You're the only ones left? You and your brothers?" The shuttle began to hum softly. Laea guessed it was the sound of the engines.

"They're not really my brothers. We just grew up together. But they might as well be brothers. We know each other much too well. And they are both a little boring."

"What happened to the other humans?" Skeeter asked.

"Many left when the war began. The rest, including my mother and father, were killed in an accident. I was very young, I don't know many details. I just know that most of the humans were killed." Laea paused, then added, "Cylons were lost as well. But they can be rebuilt."

"Hang on," Athena called. "We're good to go." She pulled back on a small wheel before her as the shuttle lifted into the air.

Into the air. Laea held her breath as the ground fell away beneath them. She wanted to laugh. She let herself smile instead.

"So where does the tour begin?" Athena asked.

Laea pointed out the window. "There's a river that runs north of the station. If you follow that for a little ways, I'll show you."

Athena turned the shuttle north. The engine made hardly any noise. Laea felt like she was swooping through the air—like a bird riding the wind.

She took a deep breath. She didn't have time for birds.

"There are other things I need to tell you," Laea said hurriedly. "Back at that staff meeting, they had things they weren't talking about."

"Like what?" Skeeter asked.

"When all the bad stuff happened, when the scavengers and the companions started to shoot at each other, two of the scavengers' ships took off, but neither of them got very far. There was another ship out here, waiting for them." She took a quick breath. "The first one—the Viper—was shot down by the new ship. The second one landed somewhere out here—so it wouldn't get shot down, is my guess. It's still out here. That's where we're going."

220

"A ship was up here?" Athena asked. "What kind of ship?"

How could she answer that? "It was a big ship. Big and round. When I was little, I used to read up on Vipers and other starships. Well, actually Vin did most of the reading. I used to look over his shoulder. Maybe he could tell you what that ship was. I never saw one of those in all the programs."

"That means there's somebody else out here, too," Skeeter said.

"There were some experimental ships from the Colonies, back before the war," Athena replied. "I thought all of them had been junked. But then, I never expected to find a working research station out in the middle of nowhere."

"Could this be something the station's involved in?" Skeeter asked.

Laea paused a moment to look out the window. The river wound its way past the cultivated fields and into the trees. They were already flying over the forest.

"I don't know," she said at last. "A week ago I would have said no. But now there seem to be things the doctor and the companions aren't talking about. But there's something else. One of the pilots from the ship is still alive. That's the reason I was late for the meeting. I came out here to find him."

Athena turned to look at Laea. "Are you sure about this?"

"I think he crashed around here. I saw him—I really saw him—from a distance in the woods. I wasn't sure it was safe to talk to him. I'm afraid I got a little scared.

"I came back to the station to see if I could get some-body to go back out with me. But with both my bothers and the companions acting so oddly lately, I thought maybe it was safer to ask you." She looked down at the chair she sat in and grinned. "I didn't know I'd get to fly in one of these things, besides."

She frowned as she looked back at the forest rushing by below. "I don't know if I can tell exactly where I saw him."

It was difficult from the air to tell exactly where she had traveled on the ground. She could see the river clearly enough, except in those places where the forest grew too thick to see the ground beneath.

She craned her neck around to glance out another window, trying to see where they were in relation to the station. Hadn't they gone far enough by now?

She turned her attention forward and saw a flash of metal down below.

She pointed at the spot. "There! Try down there!"

Athena quickly landed the shuttle in a clearing by the riverside.

"This stranger, this scavenger," Laea continued quickly, scared, she guessed, that they would find him before she could finish her story, "he might have been as surprised by me as I was by him. He called out, though. I think he wanted to talk to me. I hope he will now.

"I hope he won't hide on us. Still, his lander should have come down somewhere nearby. Maybe if I call out to him again, he'll show up." Laea wondered if she was talking too much.

"We'll do our best to find him," Athena said as she shut down the shuttle's engines.

"You can take the straps off now," Skeeter said as he unsnapped his own restraints. "Are we likely to meet anybody else out here?"

Laea shook her head. "The companions rarely leave the station. Occasionally Epsilon will form a hunting party to bring back food for the humans. But with the recent crisis, everybody's back at the station."

They all climbed out of the shuttle. This time, Laea led the way.

The forest around them was very quiet.

"I saw a flash of metal, back this way." Laea headed back the way the shuttle had come. She took a path along the river's edge. Within fifty steps, they had turned a corner and lost sight of their ship.

She stopped abruptly. "I hear something ahead," she said softly. There it was again, the snap of a twig, the sound of someone pushing his way through the underbrush.

"Whoever it is isn't even trying to be quiet," Athena whispered. "Do you have many animals here?"

"Native to the planet?" Laea shook her head. "There are very few. Birds and rodents, mostly. And I think the research station brought the rodents." She saw a break in the trees ahead.

"I see another clearing. Maybe we can get a good look at this scavenger."

They moved closer to the next open space, being careful to stay just inside the tree line.

"Over there!" Athena pointed. "Something's shiny."

"Maybe our friend's carrying a gun," Skeeter replied.

Laea heard another branch break, followed by the whir and clank of gears.

A dark metal machine stepped into the clearing.

"Holy frak!" Skeeter whispered. "It's a toaster!"

Maybe, Laea realized, she hadn't seen the stranger's lander. Maybe the glint had come from the metal body of a companion.

The machine turned to look at them. Half of Laea wanted to stand up and identify herself, to ask what business the companions had in the forest. But the other half of her saw something else.

This companion was a stranger, too.

CHAPTER
20

Skeeter saw a Cylon. No, he told himself, they were called "companions" here.

"Hey!" he called to Laea. "I thought you said there wouldn't be any companions this far out."

Laea frowned at the machine on the far side of the clearing. "I don't think I've ever seen this companion. I mean, it's a Warrior—one of the new Centurion models. Except, see the way that red light flashes behind its visor? That's different. That's not one of ours."

The strange machine lifted its arms. The machine held a weapon.

"Watch out!" Athena cried as a bright red beam sliced across the open space.

All three of them ducked behind the trees as the machine turned slightly, taking aim at their new position.

"Frak!" Skeeter whispered from where he crouched. "We've got ourselves a *real* Cylon this time!"

The forest would give them some cover. But the area behind them was filled with thick bushes. Skeeter thought he saw some brambles, too. They would make far too much noise trying to escape that way.

"How can this happen?" Laea demanded indignantly. "We've never seen Cylons here—I mean *real* Cylons—before!"

"That you know about," Athena reminded her. "Remember you said you thought the companions were keeping secrets?"

"They've been talking to Cylons?" Her tone of voice said she couldn't believe it.

"We probably now know who owns that big ship that shot the Viper out of the sky," Skeeter added.

"You mean the companions knew about the ship? They hid it from us?"

"We don't know that for sure," Athena replied softly.

"It's just damn well likely," Skeeter added. He peeked around the corner of the tree. "Sooner or later, that thing's going to figure out we're unarmed."

Red beams shot out suddenly from across the clearing—a dozen in rapid succession. Branches came crashing down from overhead, some quite close to their hiding place. Skeeter's nostrils were filled with the smell of charred wood.

"I think it already knows," he added. "That thing is going to kill us."

"We have to get back to the shuttle and warn the others," Athena said.

Skeeter looked at her. "Well, at least some of us do."

He could hear his grandmother's words filling his head.

You don't go to bed on time
You don't stop making noise
You don't wash behind your ears
The Cylons are gonna get you!

Guess he was going to end up a naughty boy after all.

"I'll distract the thing!" Skeeter whispered hoarsely. "You head back to the river!"

He jumped out from behind the trees before anyone could object, yelling and waving his arms as he tried to head in the opposite direction from the others.

He didn't make it two steps before he felt a searing pain in his arm. All his breath left him as he fell to the ground.

"Skeeter!" Athena shouted.

He groaned. Frak, did that hurt.

"It got me in the shoulder," he whispered as Athena crawled to his side. His right shoulder. He looked over at the wound. It seemed like there was an awful lot of blood.

"It's coming toward us!" Laea shouted. Skeeter raised his head enough to see that the machine was marching straight at them across the field.

Laea glanced at Athena. "Maybe I can distract it while you get Skeeter back to the ship."

Skeeter shook his head. "We already tried that one. We didn't come out here to get you killed."

The young woman kept her eyes on the machine. "I know my way around these woods. If I can avoid that thing, I can double back out of here and make it to the station in a couple of hours."

A bolt of red light barely missed Laea's head.

"I don't think any of us are going anyplace!" Skeeter shouted.

They all ducked when they heard a huge boom.

Skeeter looked up. The lower two-thirds of the Cylon still stood some twenty paces distant.

But the Cylon's head was gone.

The machine fell to the ground an instant later.

Skeeter tried to stand up and take a look around.

"Who did that?" he demanded.

A man wearing torn, soiled clothes waved at them from the far side of the clearing.

"That would be me."

Skeeter realized that standing was not a good idea. He looked down at his hands. Where had all this blood come from?

His eyes closed as he fell back down.

Laea watched the stranger as he kicked at the still machine. The Cylon. Then Skeeter collapsed.

Laea turned to Athena. "Is he . . . ?"

"He's badly hurt. We'd better get him back to the shuttle."

The stranger walked across the clearing, a large rifle in his hand. He nodded to Laea, then smiled.

"I'm Tom Zarek, and I think we almost met before."

Laea nodded back. This time, he had his shirt on. It was torn and stained, but it still covered most of his torso. Maybe she could talk to him now.

"I'm sorry about what happened before," she said quickly. "I saw your ship fall back to the ground. I went looking to see if anybody had survived."

She felt herself growing hot. She took a deep breath. "I'm apparently not that good at talking to strangers."

"I'm glad we had another chance to get together. So what happened to the man I saw before?" It was only then that the newcomer noticed Skeeter on the ground, his arm covered with blood. "Frak! The toaster shot somebody?"

Athena looked up from where she had torn off a length of cloth from Skeeter's dry sleeve to wrap around the wound. "Yeah. Got him in the arm. If we can stop the bleeding, I think he'll be all right."

"You're Colonial fleet," Tom Zarek said. He shook his head. "I never thought I would be so glad to see you. But then I never thought we would have a Cylon problem."

"And who are you?" Athena asked as she tied the bandage tight.

"Well, I was a raider on the cruiser *Lightning*, but I think I've recently retired. I didn't like the job all that much after I got it."

He sighed and glanced back at the Cylon. "I'm not so proud of what's gone on here the last couple days. I was supposed to get our pilots returned to us. Instead, I managed to just barely duck out of a fight. I've mostly just been waiting to be rescued. I hope you can oblige. Especially since I think the Cylons are looking for me."

Skeeter groaned. He was waking up!

"Why would there be Cylons here?" Athena asked sharply. "Do you know?"

"I think they were here long before the *Lightning* showed up. I tried to run, but there was another ship. Biggest ship I ever saw. I bailed before it could shoot me down."

Athena nodded, glancing at Laea. "So she told us."

Zarek pointed at the smoldering remains in the middle of the field.

"Current evidence suggests that big ship was Cylon." Zarek looked up and down the clearing. "I have the feeling that toaster isn't alone. And we just made a big noise that might well attract the others."

Athena hoisted the other pilot up to lean against her shoulder. "Can you walk?" she asked. He managed to nod. She turned to the others.

"I'm getting Skeeter back to the ship."

They hobbled together back toward the river.

Laea didn't move. She looked straight at Tom Zarek. He was tall and thin. His dark hair fell just over his ears, and his eyes seemed to look right through her. He really was very good looking. Maybe that was what made her stomach feel funny.

"Come with us," she said.

"And leave all this behind?" He glanced down at his rifle. "I think you've convinced me. Whatever you've got has to be better than Cylons."

"Watch out!" Athena called from the other side of the clearing.

Two more red flashes came out of the woods on the

far side of the field. Both hit the trees just above their heads. Laea and Tom fell to the ground as Athena pushed Skeeter behind a tree.

But Laea had gotten separated from the others. They were more than twenty paces apart, across the open field. The Cylons would kill anyone who stepped out in the open.

"Get out of here!" Laea called. "We'll find our way back overland!"

Athena nodded. "I'll get Skeeter back to the ship!" She dragged the wounded man farther back into the trees.

Zarek fired a round in the general direction of the Cylon's blasts. He waved to his right.

"Go back into the trees. Run, that way! My ship's just out of sight. I'll cover you!"

He fired back at the tree line three more times.

Laea sprinted into the woods. She saw a patch of silver in front of her. It was the lander, just down a short path. As she ran closer, she saw that the ship was sitting at an odd angle atop a pile of tree limbs it had gathered on its way down. She heard Zarek's gun blast away behind her—three times—then heard his running feet crashing through the underbrush.

"I'm right behind you!" he called. "The door's on the other side!"

She half ran, half climbed through the debris to reach the far side of the lander. The hatch stood open.

Tom was right at her back. "Get inside!" He turned and fired again and she stepped inside.

It was dark in the lander, the only light coming from

some small windows half-covered by branches. The back half of the small space was lost in shadow. There was still enough light, however, to see a large pile of guns in the middle of the floor.

Tom jumped in after her, slamming the door shut behind him.

"We can get some lights in here if you want," he said. "I was saving the ship's battery in the hope I might get a signal out. Now that somebody's found us, I don't have to worry about the wireless."

Laea heard a series of sharp pings, like the sound of pebbles hitting the ship's outer skin.

Zarek frowned. "I think the hull of this thing is good against small-weapons fire. But we're easy targets here. I killed one Cylon, but now I'm guessing we've got two more. But that's just the beginning. That ship was big enough to hold thousands."

Laea flinched as more pops rattled against the hull. "Shouldn't we wait here? If there's a Battlestar out there, can't they save us?"

"I'm sure they can, and I'm sure they will. We just don't know how long it's going to take them to get back here. I'm also sure that the Cylons have plenty of weapons that could cut this ship in two. We need to find someplace that isn't quite so exposed."

He walked over to the center of the lander's cabin and started to pick through the guns. "I know a cave where we can make a better stand. It's not far off—on a ridge a few hundred klicks to our west. We should be able to see the rescue party and defend ourselves."

Laea looked out the nearest window. She saw nothing but trees. "But that means we've got to get out of here."

"Well, we have the firepower." Tom kicked gently at the pile. "Ever handle a gun?"

Laea nodded. "My brothers and I used to take target practice out at the edge of the cultivated fields. I've never shot at a moving target, though."

"Well, I think you're going to get your chance. We'll have to gather up enough guns, ammo, and supplies to last us for a couple of days, and just hope that's enough time for the others—"

Laea put her hand on Tom's arm. "Did you hear that?"

He nodded, and pointed toward the sound. Something was moving in the shadows at the far side of the lander.

Zarek raised his rifle and pointed it at the darkness.

A man, dressed all in black, stepped into the light. He pointed a handgun directly back at Zarek's head.

The newcomer grinned. "Come on now, Tom, we don't want to make a mess."

"Creep!" Tom replied.

"That's what they call me."

If Tom Zarek was thin, this newcomer was downright emaciated. His skin was almost as pale as Gamma's white enamel. He had sunken cheeks and thinning hair. The hand that held the gun shook a bit. He did not look at all healthy.

His gaze flicked to Laea.

"Nice of you to bring company." He looked back at Tom. "And nice of you to leave me behind." He took a step closer.

"Where were you?" Zarek demanded. "By the time I got into the lander, Boone was dead. But I couldn't see you anywhere!"

The Creep shrugged. "Let's say I took a step away from the fighting. I can tell when the odds are against me. There's a reason the Creep never gets caught." He lifted his gun slightly, so it was aimed over Tom's head. "So, maybe part of the fault lies with me."

Zarek kept his rifle aimed at the other man. "If I had had you with me to shoot our guns, we might have taken out a Cylon or two. We might have gotten out of here!"

The Creep grinned. It made his face look like a skull. "So we both made mistakes. You keep on making them— leaving that door open. What say we start fresh? I'll put down mine if you'll put down yours."

Tom slowly lowered his rifle. The Creep carefully returned his handgun to a holster at his side.

The Creep stared at Laea. "You haven't introduced me to your friend. You know that raiders always share whatever they find." He glanced back at Tom. "But I heard your speech back there. About blasting your way out of here and making for that cave. I think that plan would work better if you had three people fighting the Cylons. So let's get our supplies together, shall we?"

He paused to look at Tom and Laea in turn. "We can all catch up when we get to the cave."

CHAPTER

21

Adama realized there would be no easy answers. He felt as though the doctor, and perhaps all the humans in this place, wanted so desperately for the facility to survive that they had even stopped looking at the questions. He supposed everyone had parts of their lives that were so difficult that they were hard to look at. He had his own problems trying to balance his work with the needs of his family—problems he was probably still trying to run away from. But he hoped his family problems would never reach beyond some simple misunderstandings.

Misunderstandings here seemed to end in destruction and death.

The young woman, Laea, had seemed to know that something was wrong, and had wanted to help. He wondered if she would be able to show Athena and Skeeter anything that could explain the complexities of this place.

He supposed he could talk to everyone over this grand dinner the doctor had planned. And after that, all they had to determine was what to do with the prisoners from the raider vessel, the human survivors of the station, and close to one hundred somewhat modified Cylons.

Everyone had left the meeting together, all going to see the prisoners. They had walked in a line along a series of long hallways. Gamma led the way, followed by Jon and Vin, and then the doctor, quite spry despite his frail appearance, flanked by Epsilon and Beta. Adama and Tigh were happy to bring up the rear. It gave them a chance to get a good look at all the parts of the station they were passing through—not that there was that much to see in these featureless hallways. But it also gave them the opportunity to talk a bit in low tones without any of the others appearing to notice.

"Why didn't they tell us about the prisoners sooner?" Tigh whispered.

"I think they didn't want to. Maybe the doctor did. But he seems overwhelmed. I think he might genuinely want to leave here and go back to the Colonies."

"So he's happy we're here."

"Yeah. But I'm thinking he might be the only one."

"Who can tell with these 'modified' Cylons?" Tigh shook his head. "I think once a toaster, always a toaster."

Adama still hoped he was wrong.

"The station hospital is just ahead," the doctor called over his shoulder. "The prisoners, to my understanding, are right through here."

"They have been well taken care of," Gamma added.

"We have sufficient programming to provide for most basic human needs."

Adama and Tigh stepped into a large and mostly empty room. Only one corner of the space, hidden by curtains, seemed to hold any activity. The humans and companions walked across the cavernous space, their feet echoing in the emptiness.

Epsilon stepped forward and pulled aside the curtains. "Here are your pilots."

The prisoners lay in two hospital beds, side by side. Their eyes were closed, their arms connected by wires to a number of machines, all of which beeped or hummed softly. The pilots were perfectly still, barely breathing.

"I'm afraid we didn't know what to do with them," the doctor said. "This seemed to be the best solution."

"We have instructions to treat the severely wounded thus," Gamma continued, "to wait for the next supply ship. When the station was fully functional, we would receive supply ships on a regular basis. They would have the medical supplies and expertise to help the severely traumatized recover."

"What have you done to them?" Adama asked. They hardly seemed to be alive.

"They have been put into a medically induced coma," Gamma replied.

"They were unwelcome outsiders," Epsilon added. "They could not fit into our society. In this case, they became the trauma."

Tigh pointed at one pilot's bandaged arm. "What happened here?"

"He lost a hand in the fighting," Gamma replied. "We did the best we could to bandage it and stop the bleeding.

"I'm afraid I wasn't very close to the action," the doctor admitted. "I didn't even realize the extent of their injuries."

Again, Adama thought, *Or you didn't really want to know.*

"What has happened to their Vipers?" Adama asked.

Beta spoke up. "There is much we lack. We have begun to strip them down for parts."

Adama wondered, if they could find something useful in the pilots, if they might take them apart as well. But no, these "companions" had done what was necessary for their survival. Were they able to make rational decisions? Or was this all part of their programming?

Adama looked at the assembled men and machines. "We will arrange for the disposition of these men. We have the facilities on *Galactica* to help them heal—and to keep them under lock and key until we find out just what they know." He turned to Saul. "Captain Tigh. Find out from our hosts here if we can transport them in their current condition. I'm going to talk to the admiral and see who else we can get down here to help."

"Would you like to use our comm center?" Jon asked.

Adama shook his head. "I'll just make a quick call from my ship. *Galactica* is already monitoring the shuttle's frequency. They'll be waiting for my call." He looked back at the door they had come through. "Is there an easy way to get from here to the landing field?"

Vin waved at the far side of the curtains. "Actually, if

you go farther this way, you'll come right out on the far side of the field. I'll be glad to show you."

All the corridors in this place made it seem a bit like a maze. It was obviously designed for a much larger staff. The more Adama saw of this facility, the more he realized this might have been a worthwhile project—except it was far too little and far too late. The Cylon problem had erupted before they could even get this venture properly under way. But in studying man/machine interaction, the work they had done on Research Station *Omega* could still prove valuable.

"Very good, Captain. Wait for me here."

Tigh gave him a quick salute. He didn't look particularly happy to be left behind.

Adama let Vin lead the way. They left the hospital room and walked down a short hall to an even larger space—the old Viper hangar bay. Again, most of the space was empty, except for a busy area along one wall, where a trio of Cylons was carefully disassembling a pair of ancient Mark Ones. They appeared to be placing every different piece into its own separate container, each of which in turn was neatly labeled and stacked against one wall. They were saving everything for future use, just as the doctor had said.

Adama felt the slightest bit guilty leaving Tigh behind to keep the locals busy. But it would seem too odd for both of them to retreat to the shuttle. And he needed to discuss with the admiral what they were going to do, preferably in private.

Vin opened a door at the far side of the hangar, then stepped aside. "Just through here. I'll wait until you're done."

"Thank you." He appreciated that he wouldn't have to close the shuttle door in the young man's face.

He stepped out onto the field and saw that the shuttle was gone. Adama almost turned around to confront Vin about the disappearance. The two Vipers were where they had left them, however. If the "companions" were going to take any of their ships, wouldn't they take all of them? There must be another explanation. He walked quickly over to the nearer of the two Vipers. He reached inside and powered up the wireless.

"Adama to *Galactica*."

"*Galactica* here."

"You don't happen to know the whereabouts of our shuttle?"

"*Athena took it out, Colonel. She said she had your permission.*"

"Oh." Adama felt a sudden surge of relief. Apparently, his pilots were taking the quick way to track down whatever Laea wanted to show them. "Well, then I guess she does have permission. Put me through to the admiral."

A moment passed before he heard the admiral's voice.

"*Sing here.*"

"Admiral. I'm away from the others. I can talk freely."

"*What's your assessment of the situation?*"

Adama decided to be blunt. "I think we got here just

before this whole place fell apart. It's already crumbling around the edges. And while the Cylons on this station do not seem to be combatants, they have been showing some worrisome tendencies. They've got two prisoners here from the scavenger ship that they've put into comas. I want to get these men on *Galactica* as soon as possible to see if they can tell us anything."

"*We'll send down a med team,*" Sing agreed. "*Other recommendations?*"

"Something has to be done here with the human staff. The old man at least looks like he could use medical attention. I'm not sure about the youngsters."

And what would happen if they brought the humans back? He didn't think anyone would want to leave the facility under the control of Cylons—modified or not.

Perhaps they could maintain the facility here until the original researchers on Picon could send replacements.

It was a controlled situation, one laboratory setting on one world very far away from the Colonies.

But he imagined Colonial citizens would be outraged if they knew anything about it. Supporting a site with Cylons? Too many people had lost too much in the war. The researchers here would be branded as traitors. No one could understand a place where man and machine could live in peace.

If that was, indeed, the true nature of this place.

"*Colonel?*" Sing prompted.

"Sorry, sir. I was thinking what we might do in the long term with this place. Even though they seem to be cooperative, I don't know if we can trust these Cylons' continuing motives. We may need to shut the whole thing down. I'm not sure the Cylons would agree. We'd probably need at least a major force from the *Galactica* to get them to comply. It might get complicated."

"*Understood,*" Sing replied. "*I'll talk to the fleet. I'm guessing this facility is still under Picon jurisdiction. It will be up to them to decide.*" The admiral paused, then added, "*But that means talking to Colonial governments. That never goes quickly. I imagine it will take a few days to come to a decision. Are you comfortable with staying at the facility?*"

"I think that's for the best. I believe I've gained their trust. We'll stay here, tell them we've contacted their home government. See if they might want to send any messages of their own back to Picon. After the med team retrieves the prisoners, I think it's best if just the four of us stay as our official representatives. The station seems in a fragile balance. The fewer new elements introduced into their lives at this point, the better.

"I'll know more about the situation here after I get a report from Athena and Skeeter. They're out taking a look around."

"*I understand they checked in with* Galactica *when they first went out,*" Sing replied. "*We haven't heard back from them yet. We've been getting periodic interference with our signals up here, both wireless and dradis. I wanted to ask you about that. Is there anything down there you think can be causing this interference?*"

"Nothing I've seen, or they've told me about. Could

there be some other cause?" Adama knew that storms and large magnetic fields had disrupted signals in the past.

"Nothing natural, as far as we can tell. I've got the techs working on it. But stay alert!"

"Yes sir!"

"Hopefully Athena will check in soon. Talk to me again after you've spoken with her.

"Sing out." The admiral broke the connection.

So they would have a couple more days to look around here before the ultimate decision was passed down from the Colonies. Adama was relieved it was out of his hands.

He supposed it was time to go back and get ready for dinner.

Athena heard the big boom of Zarek's gun as she helped Skeeter back to the shuttle. The other pilot was able to walk, after a fashion, as long as she didn't rush him too much. Her temporary bandage had stanched most of the flow, but Skeeter was still leaving a trail of blood all along the river path. It seemed to take forever to get him back to the level spot where she had parked the shuttle. She saw the small ship at last, twenty paces from the forest's edge. She had to get him across the clearing as quickly as possible.

"Come on Skeet, we're almost there."

"I'm with you. I'm with—" He grunted in pain.

They crossed the field without incident. She struggled him through the hatch and into the copilot's seat. She checked the view through the windows as she powered up their transportation. It was all quiet out there. She couldn't see any Cylons after them—yet.

"Feels good to sit down," Skeeter managed after a moment.

"I'll get us back to the *Galactica*."

Skeeter tried to smile. "Sounds good to me. I'll just sit back and enjoy the view."

"You do that. In the meantime, I think we have a little news to share with home."

She tried to raise *Galactica* as she made the final preparations for liftoff. All she got was a burst of static.

Athena frowned. "Well, I guess we've got to get out from under these trees." She engaged the engines and grabbed the wheel. "Hang tight, Skeets."

She lifted off, and started climbing toward the upper atmosphere. Smooth sailing so far. When she got a little higher, she'd try to raise *Galactica* again.

"Athena!" Skeeter pointed above her head. "We're being followed!"

She looked to where he pointed at the dradis screen above the front window. There was some sort of small craft in close pursuit. It looked like some kind of modified Viper, longer and sleeker than the models on the *Galactica*. Her guess was this was the special Cylon model.

"I'm sorry, Skeeter. You're going to have to hang on. We've got to shake our tail."

The shuttle didn't have the same flexibility or speed

as a Viper. Usually. She'd just have to ignore that and pretend it did. She rose quickly, then banked to the right. The Viper was gaining on them.

"Frak!" Skeeter swore. "No way you can outrun something like that."

"So we'll just have to outfox them. Maybe we'll have to wait a bit to get back to *Galactica*. I think we need to take this news straight to Colonel Adama."

Athena knew they had hospital facilities at the research station. They could fix something as simple as a shoulder wound.

"Watch it!" Skeeter shouted. "That baby's gonna climb up our rear exhaust!"

"Only if we invite it in. Which we're not."

She dropped suddenly, skimming the shuttle just above the trees.

The Viper overshot its intended target, shooting far overhead, then arced around to follow.

Skeeter stared at the dradis screen. "We can't do this forever! We have to have weapons! We're slow and clunky! The Viper is going to get us!"

That wound was making Skeeter negative. "The Viper is not being flown by Athena," she replied. "Relax. I haven't lost a passenger yet." She didn't mention that, as a Viper pilot, she had never ever had passengers. "So shut up. I think your blood loss is making you delirious."

Skeeter shook his head and sank down in his seat. "I hope you're right."

"Oh, Athena is always right."

She flew low over the river, below the tree line, weaving with the wandering flow of water.

The Viper crisscrossed in the air above them, looking for an opening. Something exploded on the far side of the riverbank.

"They're shooting at us!" Skeeter moaned.

"And not very well. If we stay out here long enough, maybe they'll just run out of ammunition."

She looked over at the suffering Skeeter.

"That was a joke."

The Viper finally swooped down to their level, hugging the tree line some distance behind their tail.

Athena smiled. "Ah, now I've got you right where I want you."

Skeeter sat up and pointed straight ahead. "Waterfall!"

She looked up and saw a cliff face covered by a rushing torrent of water, directly in their path.

She nodded. "Just the ticket."

She banked sharply as they rushed toward the cliff. The shuttle's underside scraped the upper branches as it rose just above the rocks and trees.

The Viper crashed into the cliff face behind them, the sleek metal crumpling beneath the rushing water.

"Why did I doubt you?" Skeeter said with a weak grin.

"Hey, a Viper might be faster, but Athena's got the moves!"

"So we get to go back to *Galactica*?"

Athena shook her head. "I think if we go back up there, we're just going to gain another Viper. Hang on, and we'll go talk to Colonel Adama."

"After that, I'd trust you anywhere." He closed his eyes and groaned. "But I'd trust you more if we stopped moving around."

She nosed the shuttle slightly higher in the air, so they could see beyond the trees. The research station was dead ahead, and just in time.

Skeeter looked like he was going to pass out all over again.

People were shouting when the admiral stepped into the CIC.

"What the hell?" said Sing.

"Sir." Captain Draken looked up from his console. "We've got something big coming up on the dradis. Something really big."

"I think this is what has been interfering with our communications," the wireless operator cut in. "Excuse me, sir. They must have some sort of jamming device. Probably to keep us from seeing them."

"Granted." Sing frowned up at the great yellow disk on the dradis screen. "But why are we seeing them now?"

"I think it's a Dreadnaught, sir," someone said.

"I thought all of those were destroyed in the Cylon War," Draken replied.

"Apparently not," Sing replied.

"Who exactly is flying this thing?" Draken asked.

"They're sending us a comm signal!" the wireless officer shouted.

"Put it over the speakers," Sing ordered.

"Galactica. *This is the Dreadnaught* Invincible."

"*Invincible*," Sing replied. "We were unaware that you were still in service."

"*We are no longer a Colonial ship,*" the curiously flat voice responded. "*We were never really a Colonial ship. We have become what we were always meant to be.*

"*We are a Cylon war machine.*"

CHAPTER
22

Adama turned away from the Viper, ready to return to the others. He would relay what he and the admiral had talked about in the most diplomatic way possible. Part of him was relieved that Picon would make the final decision here. He imagined that the only solution that made sense, both fiscally and politically, would be to dismantle the station. But that would end the research, as well as the sense of human/machine cooperation that seemed to have sprung up in this odd little community.

Would any decision be the right one? He just hoped that somehow, some good might come from this place.

As he walked back toward the hangar, he saw half a dozen companions gathered just outside the door. All of them were looking up at the sky.

He turned and looked as well, to see a small golden disk, perhaps the size of a moon, hanging high above them in the sky. It was far enough overhead that he could not judge its true size.

But Adama knew its true size, and its true purpose. He recognized it, even from this distance.

It was a Dreadnaught. The largest Colonial ship ever conceived, it had been in its experimental stages when the Cylon War began. The Colonies had still managed to build three of them, and all three had turned against humankind. For the Dreadnaught was the first ship almost entirely operated by Cylons. They had designed thousands of specialized individual war machines—Cylon fighters, Cylon pilots, Cylon technicians. The Dreadnaughts all had a token human crew to supervise the Cylons—perhaps a dozen souls on each ship, without whom the ship would supposedly be unable to operate. But the heart of the ship was a vast Cylon culture, uncounted machines trained to fight so that men and women would never have to fight again.

The Colonies found, once the Cylon War began, that they had built the Dreadnaughts far too well. All three of them were under Cylon control within moments of the beginning of the war. How the Cylons had gained control of ships that supposedly were unable to operate without a human failsafe was never discovered, since none of the Dreadnaughts were ever retaken by man.

Two weeks before the war began, the fleet had asked for volunteers to man the Dreadnaught crews. Adama had been tempted, but decided he liked flying a Viper too much to shift over to a job supervising a bunch of machines. He figured, later, that that love of flying had saved his life. Three members of his crew had volunteered for Dreadnaught duty. He had never heard from any of them again.

Later in the war, he had been a part of the Battle at Gamelon Breach, where four Battlestars and three hundred Vipers had combined to bring down the Dreadnaught *Relentless*. Captain Tigh had boarded a Dreadnaught—the *Supreme*—as one of a dozen commandoes assigned to take the ship from within while the Dreadnaught's staff was busy fighting a pair of Battlestars. Tigh had barely escaped with his life when the Dreadnaught's Cylon commanders had destroyed the ship rather than let it fall into Colonial hands.

Talking about the war, back in all those bars between one port and another, both Adama and Tigh had marveled that they had faced Dreadnaughts—although many had faced them, since the war machines were involved in half a dozen of the conflict's largest battles. But Tigh would never talk about his time inside the Dreadnaught, so the conversation had moved on to other things.

The Dreadnaught *Relentless* had exploded beneath a barrage of enemy fire. The Dreadnaught *Supreme* had destroyed itself. And the last of the Dreadnaughts, the *Invincible*, or so the story went, was last seen with its engines burning, falling into a star.

The Dreadnaught was slowly growing larger above him, as though it were slowly settling toward the planet below. More companions had come out onto the landing field to watch, and Adama saw they were joined by humans as well.

He and Tigh had witnessed the deaths of two Dreadnaughts.

Now he knew the *Invincible* had escaped the fire.

Doctor Fuest approached him across the field.

"Colonel? Is this one of yours?"

"I'm afraid not, Doctor."

"Then we are both afraid. We are getting a message from the ship overhead. They wish to talk to us."

The doctor walked a few steps away and spoke briefly with a companion that Adama did not recognize. He turned back to the colonel.

"I will have a portable device brought out here for my use. Everyone on the station seems to be coming out to the field. We will all hear what they have to say."

"Doctor!" one of the companions called. "There's a smaller ship coming in!"

Adama looked to the far side of the field. It was the shuttle. Athena and the others had returned.

With a Dreadnaught in the air, who knew what other Cylon craft were patrolling overhead. Adama was glad they had made it back safely.

The shuttle landed gently midfield. Adama walked quickly over to greet it.

The hatch was thrown open as he approached. Athena stuck her head out and saw Adama.

"Colonel, Skeeter's hurt!"

She pulled her fellow pilot to her side. Adama saw that one of his sleeves was drenched with blood.

The doctor came up beside Adama. "Where's Laea?"

"We got separated." Athena shifted her weight to support the limp pilot. "She took us out there to find someone from the scavenger ship. He ended up saving our butts."

The doctor's mouth opened, as though he didn't know what else to say.

"There's more, sir," Athena added.

Adama answered for her.

"You saw Cylons." He pointed at the golden disk in the sky. "We're all going to see them shortly."

"We need to get Skeeter to the hospital."

Adama helped Athena lower Skeeter down to the tarmac. The thin pilot had no strength left to stand. The two lowered him so he could sit.

Beta was at their side, examining the wound.

"This can be easily repaired," Beta said. "I need assistance!"

Two companions with wheels—old delivery models that Adama hadn't seen before—brought a stretcher between them.

"If you would lie down here, sir, we'll get you immediate help."

"My grandmother was right," Skeeter said. "Let's go."

They rushed off with him.

"Grandmother?" Adama asked.

"He's lost a lot of blood, sir," Athena replied.

"But Laea," the doctor said at last.

"I think she's safe for now," Athena said. "We'll go back and find her soon."

. . .

Admiral Sing supposed they were in for a fight. He couldn't see a single way the Battlestar could win.

"May we speak with the one in charge?" the voice from the Dreadnaught continued.

"That would be me," the admiral replied. "Admiral Sing."

"This is a most unfortunate situation. You have stumbled upon a research project that we were hoping to maintain. There may be consequences. We are currently conferring with those above us."

"Is this a threat?" Sing asked.

"We do not deal in threats. We deal in reality. We are a much larger ship than your Battlestar. Should we deem it necessary, we could eliminate you in an instant. We see no reason at the moment for this to occur."

"The Colonies and the Cylons have signed an armistice," Sing countered. "I see no reason for either of us to fight."

"The Colonies and the Cylons are both far from this place. What happens here might never be known by either side."

Now that, Sing thought, *sounded like a threat.*

"We are currently accessing the records of Research Station Omega. *Please do nothing to interfere with our task."*

Sing looked at the others in the CIC. No one spoke. He knew some of his officers had had experience with Dreadnaughts, and there would be some pre-war schematics in their records. He wondered if this Cylon war machine would have any weaknesses.

"In our search, we discover that you have sent one William

Adama to negotiate with the research station below. Was this Adama a lieutenant during the Cylon War? Did he fly a Viper?"

Sing wondered why he was obliged to tell them anything.

"Please," the voice continued. *"Tell us what we wish to know, or we will fire upon you."*

Well, Sing supposed information wouldn't kill anyone. "Yes, Adama flew a Viper. And I believe he was a lieutenant at the time."

"Most excellent!" the voice replied. *"And he is on the planet's surface?"*

"Uh—yes," Sing answered. He hoped he wasn't signing his XO's death warrant. "Why do you want to—"

"Make no move against us, and we will make none against you. Do not attempt to use your wireless. We will be jamming your signal."

"You expect us to do nothing?" Sing demanded.

"Of course. Nothing will happen to you. Haven't the Cylons and the Colonies signed an armistice?"

Gamma brought Doctor Fuest the portable comm unit. The doctor looked at it for a moment before activating it. He had depended upon the proper functioning of machines his entire life. Why did he suddenly think this small wireless set would betray him?

He clicked the single switch to activate the unit.

"This is the Dreadnaught Invincible," a voice boomed out of the speakers located around the edges of the landing field. *"We wish to speak to* Omega."

"This is Doctor Fuest. I speak for *Omega* station."

"As we thought you would. We have accessed your station's records, and have determined your hierarchy. If we might speak to Gamma, please?"

They wished to speak to a companion? Well, Gamma was a member of the senior council. It might even know more about the station than the doctor.

"Very well, I—I suppose," the doctor managed.

Gamma stepped forward to position itself before the microphone. "Thank you, Doctor," the Butler Model said before it turned to the wireless.

"Dreadnaught *Invincible*. This is Gamma. And this is not part of our arrangement."

Arrangement? Fuest frowned. Gamma had already known of the Dreadnaught?

"Our apologies. We have made mistakes. We have tried to maintain our secrecy perhaps too diligently. In retrospect, it might have served us better to blast the recovery ship Lightning from the sky before they reached you. We did attempt to eliminate one remaining crewmember, but in so doing found ourselves looking to eliminate far many more, including one who should be protected under our original mandate. We could see no other course of action but to reveal ourselves."

What did this mean? Fuest wanted to demand an explanation from Gamma this instant. Had the other companions known about this as well?

"We now must resolve this situation in a new way. We ask that you send one of your number to the Dreadnaught to negotiate with us."

"Very well," Gamma said. "I will be willing to come aboard if I can ensure the safety of the research center."

"No, Gamma," the voice continued. *"We do not need to talk to you. We need to talk with Colonel William Adama."*

The normally stoic Adama looked stunned. He stepped forward a moment later.

"And if I do not wish to come?"

"If you do not wish to come," the voice replied, *"I cannot guarantee the safety of the research station or the Battlestar* Galactica. *If you do visit, both will be quite safe for the duration of your stay."*

Adama frowned. "Will you allow me to talk to *Galactica?"*

"They have already been informed of your impending visit."

Adama took a deep breath. "Very well. Give me a few minutes to prepare."

"Most excellent," the Dreadnaught's voice agreed.

CHAPTER
23

Laea was frightened, and not just of the Cylons.

Tom Zarek had outfitted all three of them as best he could. Each of them had a rifle and a handgun, and a large amount of ammunition that he had stuffed into three small packs he'd found in one of the lander's many compartments. The packs had also been filled with enough rations for three days and some first aid supplies from Zarek's survival kit.

He smiled at Laea as he checked his rifle. Now that the Creep was here, Tom's smile didn't warm her as much as it used to.

"Okay," Tom said. "I'll go first, and head right. The Creep will follow me and head left. If we manage to get a good position and can draw the Cylons' fire, we can cover Laea and you can get out and to a safe spot. If we can get by them, or we can shoot one of them down, maybe we can get up to the cave. I think we'll be able to defend ourselves a lot better up there until help comes."

The Creep smiled at Laea. "Hey, I'd like to cover this pretty little thing right now."

Tom grabbed the other man's coat. "You talk like that again, Creep, I'll kill you."

The Creep looked surprised. "If you can get to your gun fast enough. Hey, we're all going to die out there anyway. Can't a guy joke around a little?"

"Didn't sound much like a joke," Zarek replied.

Laea kept her distance from both men. They both seemed to hold so much violence in them—so different from the doctor and her brothers. Now that she was trapped inside a small space with these two men, she was finding their emotions more frightening than exciting. She didn't think Tom would hurt her, at least not on purpose. She tried to keep as far away from the other man as she could. He frightened her.

Not that it mattered. She thought that Tom's plan would get them all killed.

The two men stared at each other in silence for a moment.

"Have you heard the change?" she said softly.

"What change?" Tom asked.

"They've stopped firing their guns. Those little noises are gone from the hull."

The Creep grinned at that.

"She's right. Not only pretty but smart."

Somehow, the Creep made even those words sound dirty. She could see where he got his name.

"Have they left, then?" she asked.

The Creep peered out the window. "Unless they're just saving their ammunition until we come out."

"If they're gone, it's an even better time to get out of here," Tom said. "We don't know if they're gone for good. They may just be coming back here with a bigger gun."

"If they're gone," Laea said, "we might be able to get back to the research station."

"Oh that's a fine idea," the thin man replied. "Tom and I can get killed properly this time."

"No," Laea insisted. "Others have joined us. People from the Colonies. The companions have put away their guns."

"We're going to need to be rescued by somebody," Tom added. "I think Nadu is long gone."

"He seemed to give up awfully easy," the Creep replied. "Usually, Nadu won't leave the table until every scrap of meat is gone. Of course, we don't know what he was up against out there."

"Can you get us back to the base?" Tom asked.

Laea thought her only real problem would be finding her way back to the river. "As long as I can get my sense of direction from our sun, I should be fine."

"I think you've got another hour for your sense of direction, then," the Creep said. "It's almost nightfall."

"Maybe we should wait until morning," Tom suggested. "Get up to the caves before it gets dark and take a look around, see if the Cylons are really gone. If so, we can head back for your home base at first light."

Laea didn't want to spend any more time around this

Creep than she had to, but she realized Tom's plan was probably the best. They didn't want to get lost in the woods when Cylons might still be looking for them.

"All right," she said.

"Good," Tom agreed. "Then we should go as planned."

He kicked open the hatch.

Things were moving much too quickly. Doctor Fuest was never much of one for speed. But he felt he had things he must do.

He needed to be alone—or not quite alone. He walked down the empty hallways—as far as he knew, everyone from the station was still out on the field—and talked to the one he trusted most.

"Betti," he whispered.

You're troubled, Vill. I can always tell. She was there immediately. She was always there.

"Things are changing here, Betti. Things I no longer understand."

You try too hard to control everything! I've always told you, you have to learn to let go!

"Perhaps I do. The Colonies have come back to find us."

He could hear the delight in her voice. *Oh, you've wanted that for so long!*

"But the Cylons have come too, and they've been talking to the companions!"

Betti was quiet a moment before she asked. *What is it that you want, Vill?*

"I want to understand. What the companions think of me. What the Colonies want to do with our research. Everything, I guess." He thought a moment more, then added, "Someone from the Colonies is going to the Cylon ship to talk about our station. I think I need to go with them. I think I need to learn the truth."

You always know what's best, Betti replied. *Wherever you go Vill, I'm never far away.*

"I've always depended on you, Betti."

As I have depended upon you, and always will, my love.

Doctor Villem Fuest smiled.

It was good, then. He could go out and tell the others what he needed to do.

Captain Tigh couldn't believe it.

"This is madness, Bill. If you go in there, you're never coming back."

"I think that's likely," Adama agreed. "But maybe this way I'll have a chance to save the rest of you—the station and *Galactica* both. If I don't do it, I think the Dreadnaught will destroy them both."

"So you're set on this thing?" Tigh asked.

Adama nodded his head. "Yes, I am."

So be it. Tigh took a deep breath. "Well then I'm going with you."

"What?"

"Tell the toasters it's a condition for your cooperation. They want you bad enough, they shouldn't mind someone else tagging along. Remember, I've been inside one of those big boats before."

"So you've told me. But you never wanted to talk about it."

"Only because I didn't want to bring it back any more vividly than I remember it already. I remember every minute I was in that place, every day of my life."

"And you're ready to go back in there again?"

"Hey, you've backed me up in plenty of fights. It's time for me to return the favor."

"Then how can I say no?" Adama asked.

"Excuse me, gentlemen?" Doctor Fuest stepped forward from where he had been standing behind them. He had been so quiet, Tigh hadn't even realized he was there.

"Yes, Doctor?" Adama asked as if he hadn't been surprised at all.

"I would like to go to this ship as well. I would like to do it for my station."

"Thank you, Doctor," Adama replied, "but I don't think—"

"You will need me," Fuest insisted. "Out of all the humans alive, no one knows the Cylon mind better than I."

"You make a convincing case," Adama agreed. "Very well. I will state my conditions to the Dreadnaught as we prepare for takeoff."

"You know, Doctor," Tigh said softly, "none of the three of us might leave that place alive."

"Or because there are three of us," the doctor said with the slightest of smiles, "we all might survive after all."

. . .

Athena was glad to see Skeeter smile. He sat up in bed, propping his back up against the pillow. "They say I should rest, after losing all that blood. But things are happening, aren't they? These companions here don't tell me anything!"

Athena had decided it was time for visitors. Vin and Jon had come with her, and the senior companions weren't far behind.

Beta bowed slightly. "We were attempting to see that Mr. Skeeter got some rest. He should be able to move around quite freely, so long as he is careful not to do something that would open the wound. The prognosis is good for a full recovery."

"I'm glad to see you," Skeeter said to Athena. He waved at the two other beds nearby. "These guys don't do anything but sleep. So did Laea get back yet?"

Athena shook her head. "No, no one's seen her, and it's after dark."

Skeeter frowned. "Can you take the shuttle back up?"

"The shuttle's being used for something else. The Cylons have shown themselves, and they're asking to see Colonel Adama."

"And I thought I had problems. Maybe if you took one of the Vipers?"

"It wouldn't be much good now. Like I said, it's after dark. And I don't think the Cylons are very keen on having anyone do any unauthorized flying. We could end up with a new firefight on our hands while the colonel is visiting the enemy."

"Not a good idea." Skeeter struggled to come to a full

sitting position, then apparently thought better of it. He collapsed back against the pillow. "Is there any way I can help?"

"You can be our contact back here. Adama and Tigh are going to go visit the Cylon ship, along with Doctor Fuest."

"We hope that the three of them together will get the Cylons to see reason," Gamma added.

"None of us anticipated that this would happen," Epsilon agreed. "We were only thinking about the long-term safety and security of the station."

"Now I think you're trying to explain things too fast," Skeeter said. "So I'm going to be the only fleet guy left?"

"They're jamming our radio signals," Athena replied. "If the companions find any way to break through, it's up to you to contact the admiral."

"I'll do my best." Skeeter grinned again, no doubt glad to have something to do. But his smile faltered as he asked, "But how will you find Laea?"

Athena frowned in return. "I think I've got to go on foot. If I follow the river, I think I can find her easily enough."

Jon shook his head. "You're not going alone. We'll come with you."

"Hey," Vin added, clapping Jon on the shoulder, "she's our sister."

"This is our fault, too," Jon added. "We've been so busy with the station, we've been ignoring her. We should have listened to what she had to say."

Athena had heard this before. Protect the little girl, but don't listen to her. It was a big reason she had become a Viper pilot. Now people paid attention.

The companions studied each other in silence for a moment.

"Gamma and I will come too," Epsilon stated finally. "In a way, she is our sister as well."

"If Cylons still pursue her," Gamma added, "they will not expect us to take your side. It will add an element of surprise."

"We will go at dawn?" Jon asked.

"We can leave before then," Epsilon said. "We have an amphibious craft that will take us down the river, and lights to guide our way."

Athena frowned. "I don't know if I can judge the exact spot without daylight."

"Then we will wait until an hour before dawn," Epsilon replied, "so we will reach the spot just after first light. We all wish to rescue Laea. I will arrange for supplies and weapons."

"Then we will meet here one hour before dawn?" Jon asked.

Athena nodded. "We will leave from here." She looked down at the patient. "See, Skeeter? We'll keep you in on the action."

"We are almost ready to fly to the Dreadnaught," Adama said to the wireless mic.

"You say 'we,'" the voice replied. *"We only require your presence."*

"I will not come alone," Adama replied. "I will bring Captain Tigh to pilot the shuttle, and Doctor Fuest, who wishes to speak personally with those in charge aboard your ship."

The voice did not respond for a moment.

"Very well," it said at last. *"If you feel safer bringing the others, we will not deny your request. But please arrive quickly. It is important that we talk with you before we receive our final commands."*

"We will bring the shuttle now," Adama replied.

"We will allow the shuttle to approach us. Any other ship, originating on either the planet's surface, or from the deck of the Galactica, *will be shot down. We want no tricks."*

"I understand. You will get none."

"Are you prepared to leave?"

Adama glanced at both Tigh and the doctor.

"I see no reason to wait."

"Then the Dreadnaught Invincible *stands ready to welcome you."*

Adama shut off the comm controls. He glanced back at Athena.

"Skeeter knows what to tell the admiral," she said.

He nodded. "I'm looking forward to talking to all of you tomorrow."

Nobody said anything for a moment.

"I—I'm sure we will, sir," Skeeter stammered into the silence.

Adama grinned. "Stranger things have happened."

CHAPTER
24

DREADNAUGHT *INVINCIBLE*

Captain Saul Tigh remembered this place all too well: the Dreadnaught.

The thing hung in the sky like a small moon. It was close to ten times the size of the *Galactica*, its surface pockmarked with a thousand different holes—and every hole hid a different laser or missile bay or launch chute. The thing held a hundred different methods of death and destruction. Tigh remembered, when the first Dreadnaught was launched, how pleased its makers had been to come up with so high a number. It was the last excessive ship of an excessive era, just before humankind's wealth and populations were decimated by the Cylon War.

Tigh flew in through the primary chute, a hole at the very center of the monstrosity. They were not challenged or questioned. They heard no comm chatter at all.

The silence didn't help Tigh—it only reminded him that the Dreadnaught no longer held life. Now it was the home of far too many Cylons.

He set the shuttle down in a deserted hangar bay. The room was huge, almost the size of a small domed city. A hundred or more Cylon Vipers hung from cradles along the walls. They reminded Tigh of holstered weapons, just waiting to be drawn. Masses of new machinery, most of which Tigh did not recognize, sat on the floor beneath the Vipers. A lot of the equipment in here looked like it had been improved far beyond those early models he had seen in that first Dreadnaught so many years ago.

But the room was just as vast, the lighting as dim and yellow, the feeling of being very, very small just as great as it had been then.

Back in the war, his group of commandoes had commandeered a Cylon troop carrier—which the Cylons had stolen from the Colonies only a year before. They had used the carrier to land inside the Dreadnaught *Supreme*, and then started to cut their way through the Cylons.

The Dreadnaught had been a great success for the Cylons in the early years of the war, but the Cylons had apparently never devised a plan to defend their huge ship from an internal attack. The eight commandoes in Tigh's unit virtually quick-marched from the landing area to the heart of the ship, mowing down any machine they came across that might stand in their way.

That was when it got strange.

"I guess we don't get a welcoming committee,"

Adama said. Tigh snapped out of his reverie, and looked out again at the silent hangar.

"Yeah, I guess they don't want the Cylons to scare us away."

"So we won't see any Cylons at all?" The doctor sounded disappointed.

"Oh, I'm sure we'll see them sooner or later," Tigh reassured him. "They're just saving things up for a surprise."

The colonel unstrapped himself and rose from his seat. "Well, we might as well see what they've got waiting for us."

Adama opened the hatch and stepped out first. Tigh and the doctor followed. Their boot heels echoed in the vast silence that surrounded them.

"Is that Bill Adama I see?" a voice boomed from far above—a voice far different from the emotionless tones they had heard back at the research station. This voice, Tigh thought, sounded like some long-lost boisterous uncle in the middle of a holiday dinner.

"It is!" Adama called back. "And who am I talking to?"

"Oh, you'll recognize me soon enough," the voice said with a chuckle. *"I thank you for coming—all of you. But you particularly, Bill. I've got a favor to ask of you. They allow me that sort of thing, now and again. But why should I explain anything when I can show you? Follow the lighted path and all will become quite clear."*

"Well, this is different," Tigh remarked.

"The Cylons are capable of great versatility," the doctor added. "I don't think the Colonies ever fully appreciated that, before the war."

"Here's the path." Adama pointed to a row of lights

that led across the hangar to a distant corridor. More loudly, he asked, "Will we be going far?"

"Nothing's very close in this gods-forsaken ship!" the booming voice replied. *"But you'll find me soon enough. Please get on with it! I've waited far too long."*

"Apparently, the Cylon knows you?" the doctor asked.

"I think I recognize that voice," Adama replied. "And it's not a Cylon."

They moved out of the hangar, the great space as still and empty as death, and walked along an equally quiet corridor.

When Tigh had been in this place before—or the place just like this—the corridor had been crawling with machines: Cylons, not the Warriors, but all the other varieties that had fled the Colonies. None of the first machines they saw had weapons of any kind—they must have all been charged with different functions in running the massive ship. But they had tried to block the forward progress of Tigh and the others, jamming the corridors with their bright metallic forms. Too bad the commandoes had brought along the really big guns. It made for a lot of ex-Cylons.

Now the corridors were as empty as the hangar, lit mostly by the glowing lights that would lead them to their destination.

"It is nice to see you, Bill," the voice boomed from hidden speakers. *"If you don't mind, I'll entertain you with a little song."*

And the voice began to sing an old fleet song that Tigh had learned way back in basic.

"Most curious," the doctor said.

"Not curious at all," Adama replied.

It reminded Tigh of the next thing he had found, the thing not seen but heard, the thing that still haunted him, the thing he thought of every day.

It was very dark at the edge of the research station. The planet had no moon, and the stars were mostly obscured by clouds. Dawn seemed to be much more than an hour away.

Athena followed Gamma, who illuminated the path before them with a bright light the companion had revealed in its chest. The rest of their party followed, first Jon and Vin, then Epsilon taking up the rear.

All five of them carried guns large enough to disable Cylons.

"The river travels under the research station," Gamma said, "and provides us with both water and power. It emerges just ahead. I have had a small launch brought here for our use. And something else of value."

Gamma led them all down a gently sloping hill. The river emerged from a great pipe in the hillside and snaked on down through the valley below. Gamma shone his light on a boat large enough to accommodate twice their number.

"Our transportation."

The five of them quickly climbed into the boat, which was moored past a short pier. Epsilon sat in the bow. The companion's night vision capabilities would easily spot any danger. Jon untied the craft from its mooring while Vin started up the engine and gently steered the boat out into the river's current.

"We have another advantage," Gamma said to Athena. It pointed to a small white box on a central seat. "This is a tracking device. When Laea was young, she tended to wander."

"Like she doesn't wander now?" Vin asked.

"It is true," Gamma replied. "Perhaps she hasn't changed all that much. But when Laea was four, the doctor ordered that all her shoes be equipped with small chips that send out a signal. If you are within a certain distance of the chips, this box will receive the signal and show us exactly where Laea is."

"When she was young, we had to fetch her every other day," Epsilon agreed.

Athena stared down at the box. "You still place these devices in her shoes?"

"No one has ever said otherwise," Gamma replied. "And perhaps, had the senior staff paused to consider it, they might have determined that such a practice was wasteful. But today we realize that practice is not wasteful at all.

"We have not had occasion to use the tracker in years. But the chips are there now that the need arises."

Athena frowned at this new information. "With this thing, we probably could have found her in the dark."

"Possibly," Gamma replied. "But its range is only a few klicks. It was originally designed to find Laea as she ran around the station proper. We would need to be in the general vicinity for it to work properly. We still need your memories of the location to show us the way."

"It will be better to find her in daylight," Epsilon said. "She'll recognize us. It will be less frightening for her."

"And with this, we will find her quickly."

Athena stared down at the box. It was a device to protect Laea, and a device that made sure she would never really be alone. The device was reassuring and disquieting at the same time. Much like all of Research Station *Omega*.

"Ah," Epsilon announced. "The first glimmers of dawn."

Athena looked up and saw a narrow band of red over the far horizon.

Before, on the *Supreme*, Tigh remembered all too well, it had been the voices. Human voices, begging for death. Tigh and his fellows had first heard them as they passed through what had once been the officers' mess. It had once been the social center for the small human staff, but the room had been stripped of the furniture and machines and all things human that had made it a gathering place. Tigh didn't think he had ever seen another room that had looked so empty. The voices seemed to come from nowhere and everywhere. The commandoes moved forward, headed for Central Command.

The voices followed them, calling down the corridors, following their every footstep.

"Thank the gods you have found us!"

"Kill us!"

"Kill us, please!"

The commandoes had never found the source of those voices. They had thought, at first, that it was a Cylon trick, some way to distract and demoralize them until the toasters could gather together enough warriors to mount a last-ditch defense of the ship's nerve center.

Their first assumption had been wrong.

But that had been on a different ship, in a different time.

Now it was a song.

> *"Oh, I've signed up with the fleet*
> *For to go far away-o:*
> *And I'll never see my own true love*
> *Forever and a day-o!"*

Adama looked back at Tigh as they followed the lighted trail. "Is this anything like what happened before?"

"It has certain similarities," Tigh admitted.

"I see why you never wanted to talk about it," Adama agreed.

Fuest took up the rear. He seemed quietly in awe of everything around him.

"Are we getting closer?" the colonel called out to the voice.

"Oh, I've signed—why yes, Bill, you're almost there! You'll have to forgive me. I haven't felt good enough to sing in such a long time!

> *"Oh, I've signed up with the fleet*
> *For to go—"*

They kept on moving. It took Tigh a while to realize they were marching in time to the music.

"Sing here."

"We have visual confirmation, Admiral, that Adama's shuttle has landed on the *Invincible*. The Dreadnaught is still refusing to speak to us."

"Understood."

So the game continued, on the Cylons' terms. The admiral stared across his quarters without really seeing anything. Sing didn't think he had ever felt so helpless, even during the early days of the Cylon war. The *Galactica* was outgunned and had crewmembers in harm's way, and he had no way to even alert the Colonial fleet!

"Sir! We're getting new images on the dradis. Five ships—no, more than a dozen—no. Wait a moment. Sir, twenty-three ships have appeared on our screens."

Twenty-three ships? Who the hell would send twenty-three ships?

"Are they fleet? Have they sent us reinforcements?"

"Sir, this is not the fleet. Nor do I think they are Cylon craft. It is the strangest group of ships I have ever seen."

Sing stood abruptly. "I think I'd better come up and take a look."

The singing stopped abruptly.

"It's just through this door now," the cheerful voice an-

nounced. *"My old friend Bill. It will be good to see you in the flesh!"*

Adama was sure now that he knew who was speaking, even though he hadn't seen him in close to thirty years.

"Chief Nedder? Is that you?"

"Right the first time! You always were a bright fellow."

The door in front of the three swung open.

They walked into another empty room. A tall, ornate set of doors dominated one wall. They looked to Adama like the sort of cupboards people used to store things in back on Caprica.

"Almost there!" Chief Nedder's voice cheered. *"But before I truly introduce myself, I should ask you, Bill, who'd you bring for company?"*

Tigh stepped forward. "Captain Saul Tigh. I'm Bill's crewmate."

"He's a good friend, too, Ned," Adama added.

"Ah, I had few better friends than Bill, back in the day. And who's the other one?"

The doctor looked up. "Villem Fuest. Doctor Villem Fuest. I come from the research station below. I've worked with Cylons—or the descendants of Cylons—all my life. I've come to see what these Cylons can do."

"Well, I can certainly show you that. It's the moment of truth, Bill."

"Where are you, Ned?"

"You see those fancy doors? Take a deep breath and open them. I warn you, though. I'm no longer a pretty sight."

Adama opened the doors.

"Frak," Tigh murmured in a voice just loud enough to hear. The doctor gasped.

Adama saw the head of his old friend, crew chief on his very first ship. But while his face was recognizable, most of the rest of his body was gone, replaced by tubes and wires. The face in the middle of the machine grinned. A metal rod with a human hand on its end made a mock salute.

"This is me now," said the thing that had once been Chief Nedder. "Welcome to my world."

"The Cylons did this to you?" Doctor Fuest asked.

"They had to," Nedder explained. "I'm a necessity.

"The Colonies were far too clever. Or they thought they were. The Dreadnaughts would only operate with their human staffs in control. Or, as the Cylons determined, having the appearance of control. They needed my human parts to run their ship. The pattern of a living eye to activate the weapons system, the warmth of a living handprint to run the engines. As you see, they've kept the parts they needed and made sure the rest of me wouldn't go anywhere."

Adama had never seen anything like this. Half man, half machine. The fact that this had once been his friend made it even more of an abomination. "God, Ned, how can you bear it?"

The chief laughed at that. "I've gone mad from the pain and come back again. You see, you have to be at least a little sane to find a way to kill yourself.

"They use me to control the ship, but I still have a wee

bit of free will. I can shut them down at inopportune moments. It pays to let me have the occasional favor.

"You, Bill Adama, are such an occasional favor."

The chief cackled again.

"The Cylons are always lying to you about one thing or another. They have plans. Big plans. Not that they'd share any of them with me. But I don't want to be a part of those plans.

"I can turn myself off for brief periods. They always bring me back. A painful affair.

"But they wouldn't want me to do something to interfere with their operations, especially when they're facing a Battlestar. In order to keep working for them, I asked for an hour with you. And in that hour, you will kill me."

Nedder laughed one more time.

It was Adama's turn to look up at the featureless walls. "How can you tell us this? Aren't the Cylons listening in?"

"I am the Central Control of all the systems," the chief replied. "For a little while, I can keep them out.

"Killing me will disable the ship. They'll be floating free in space. I know they have plans to jury-rig something if I die, but that will take time. I'll open every door on this boat as my last command. You and the *Galactica* will be far away from here before they can retaliate. They won't be able to do a thing against you."

Adama nodded.

"What do you want me to do?"

"A couple quick cuts to sever my works. I—"

A warning siren came from somewhere.

"What?" Nedder cried. "Someone's attacking! Looks like our meeting's over." The chief stared at Adama.

"You wouldn't have done this to me, Bill?"

Adama frowned. "I wouldn't. But I don't control *Galactica*." Would Sing have ordered a sneak attack? It didn't sound like the admiral's style.

The chief's eyes half closed. "I can hear our Vipers responding to it already. It sounds like a bit of a battle."

Cylon Warriors appeared on either side of them.

Where the hell did they come from?

"Can't you tell them this isn't our doing?" Adama asked.

"Ah, Bill," Nedder replied. "To the Cylons, all humans are responsible.

"I'm afraid my time is up, and so is yours. I'm hoping we can finish our business later. I'll try to talk to them.

"But then, my employers are not the most forgiving types."

The chief laughed one final time as the three men were taken away.

CHAPTER
25

Nadu was laughing.

"You never expected this, you Cylon scum!"

Griff never thought his captain would pull this off. He had called in all his debts and favors, even threatened a few of the other ships' captains with a bit of blackmail, but he had gathered twenty-three recovery ships, Nadu's own small avenging navy.

And now all twenty-three ships were attacking the Cylon Dreadnaught.

"Steal from Nadu, will you? No one gets the better of Nadu! Even the Cylons are going to pay!"

His captain had always been half-mad. Now Griff thought he had gone all the way.

Grets looked over from the dradis screen, where she

was filling in for one of their lost crewmembers. "They're launching a counterattack. Vipers!"

"We can handle a few Vipers. We have twenty-three ships, with seventy-eight fighters. How many Vipers do they have?"

Grets looked back at the dradis screen. "I would say hundreds."

"We'll fight them all!"

Griff winced as he saw their first fighters explode under an onslaught of never-ending Cylon craft. The Captain was laughing again. He had run once. He would never run again.

"Death to Cylons!" Nadu called.

Griff was beginning to fear it would be the other way around.

Admiral Sing watched the strange drama play out beyond the *Galactica*. They had pulled the ship into a higher orbit to make sure they kept out of the fight.

"Our wireless channels are free, sir."

Apparently, the Cylons had found a distraction.

"Send a priority message to the fleet. 'Have encountered Cylons. Need immediate assistance.'"

"Aye, sir!"

"Can we talk with the research station?" Sing asked.

"I'll put you through as soon as we've sent your priority to the fleet."

"Sir! Should we take any retaliatory action?"

Sing frowned at the Vipers pouring out of the Cylon

ship. How could he take sides against the Dreadnaught when he had two officers on board?

Laea woke up with a hand across her mouth. Early morning light seeped into the cave. And the Creep stared down at her from a foot away.

"You won't ignore me any longer." He grinned. "Zarek's looking around, seeing if it's safe for us to leave. So we've got a few minutes."

He took his hand off her mouth. "He's not going to hear you scream. Especially now that it's doomsday."

Laea was more startled than afraid. She thought maybe the whole universe had gone mad. "What?" she demanded. "What are you talking about?"

He grabbed her arm and dragged her to the edge of the cave.

"Look in the sky. It's the end of all of us."

She looked up and saw a dozen different dots high in the sky, swarming around the golden disk she had seen the day before. A couple of the dots vanished in brilliant explosions of light.

"It's the Cylon War, all over again," the Creep said. "We're never going to make it out of here alive. So I thought we could at least enjoy our last few minutes." He reached down to undo his belt.

"I'd stop there," Tom's voice said from behind them. "Do you really think I'd leave you alone with her for more than a minute?"

She looked around to see Tom's gun pointed straight

at the Creep. "I went up on the ridge. I think we've got a clear path back to the river. I say we get ourselves back to *Omega*."

Laea pushed herself to her feet. Yes! She hadn't realized how much she missed the station until the last few hours.

She pointed to the Creep. "Why do you keep including him in our plans? How can you trust him, Tom?"

"We need every gun we have," the Creep replied. "That's why I don't kill Tom, and he doesn't kill me. I still think you should give me a moment. Heck, we could take turns."

Zarek took a step closer. "Creep, if you make another move toward—"

But the Creep was already moving. He knocked the gun from Zarek's hand and kicked him in the crotch. Zarek crumpled to the cave of the floor. When he looked up, the Creep had his gun pointed at him.

"You've got potential, Tom. Too bad you'll never live to use it!" His skull face grinned. "You've got a choice. I can kill you now, or you can sit and watch. I've waited long enough to get what I need."

"And you will wait longer still," a deep voice interjected.

The Creep whirled around. "Frakkin' Cylons!"

"Epsilon!" Laea cried. "You found me!"

"We always find you," Epsilon replied.

"I can kill a Cylon with this!" the Creep screamed. "I know a spot! I just shoot you in the neck!" He pointed his gun forward, and began to squeeze the trigger.

He staggered back at the sound of a shot. He looked down and saw the blood spread across his chest.

"Who?" the Creep asked.

Athena stepped into the cave. "Epsilon came with friends." She smiled at Laea. "See? I knew we'd get you out of here after all."

The three humans were placed in another room, as featureless as all the corridors they had passed through. Apparently, Adama thought, Cylons needed neither decorations nor furniture.

The same voice they had heard over the wireless boomed from somewhere overhead.

"I am disappointed in you, Colonel Adama."

"Why?" Adama asked. "Because there is a battle going on outside this ship that I know nothing about?"

"You heard Chief Nedder. To Cylons, all humans are responsible."

"So you were listening in?"

"Of course. Once, the Chief could block our entry. But we have rerouted the systems. Now we can monitor his every action."

"So you know he wants to die?"

"We've known that for many years. You will not be there to assist him. Nor you—Captain Tigh, isn't it?"

"Frak you!" Tigh shot back.

"For Cylons, that is not yet possible," the voice replied. "But Doctor. We are surprised to see you here."

"Really?" The doctor blinked as though he was equally surprised. "You know that I have spent my entire life studying Cylons, and the interaction of humans and Cylons? This seemed to be the chance of a lifetime."

"Most interesting. Doctor, how would you like a tour of our ship?"

"I would very much like that, thank you."

"And we would like to talk to a human as different as you. As to our two military men, I'm afraid you will have to remain here."

The voice paused, then added, *"If it will help the chief to function, we may yet let you live."*

The door opened. An armed Centurion watched them from the corridor outside.

"Doctor, if you would?" the Cylon voice said.

The doctor leaned close to Adama and whispered in his ear.

"Do not mourn me."

Fuest looked apologetically at the other two and left the room.

The Cylons had done wonders. The ship was huge, with more than a dozen different decks, all full of working machines. The Cylons not only maintained the ship, but seemed to be constantly improving every system on board. The voice guided the doctor from station to station, while the two warriors who formed his escort kept a respectful distance. He saw machine shops for both repair and manufacture of new models, a whole floor dedicated to experimental dradis and communication systems, even what the voice referred to as a "strategic preparations room," where two dozen Cylons had literally plugged their operating systems into a central core. The doctor found the variations fascinating, and so different from the direction his own companions had taken back on the station. It was a shame, really, that an intelligence like this and the cultural wealth of humanity could not find a way to work together.

He shared his thoughts with the voice of the ship, and the ship seemed pleased. But perhaps that was an old man's fancy as well.

"We have accessed the records of your home, recorded all your experiments," the voice said as they returned to the ship's primary level. *"We would let you see our home as well."*

A moment later, the voice added, *"We are interested in your reaction."*

"A human reaction?" the doctor asked.

"Both Cylons and humans come from the same place," the voice replied. *"But perhaps that is a discussion for another day."*

"Well, you have done wonderful things. Made strides far beyond anything I've seen in the companions. But you don't need me to tell you that, do you?"

The voice did not reply.

The doctor looked up the corridor they had just entered. "We have come full circle, haven't we? The chief would be just beyond those doors?"

"You have a sense of direction worthy of a Cylon, Doctor."

This hall featured an empty shelf along one wall, a shelf that had once no doubt held something valuable to humans.

The doctor pointed at the shelf. "I am quite tired. May I sit awhile?"

"Of course."

Fuest took a deep breath. He needed to have a final conversation.

"Betti," he said softly.

Yes, Villem, I am always here.

"You have seen everything."

Everything. The good and the bad.

"The bad," he agreed.

Yes, that is something that humans and Cylons were never meant to do.

He nodded. "I knew you'd understand, Betti. About my decision. It may be the last thing I ever do."

You were always a brave man, Vill. And if it is the last thing, then we shall be together.

"Yes we will, won't we?"

The thought brought great comfort.

"What is it that you say?" the voice boomed from above.

"I am an old man now. I was talking to my wife. I keep her with me." Fuest smiled. "I don't know if Cylons would understand that."

The voice paused. *"Maybe we will never understand the ways of humans."*

"Maybe you don't need to. You have distanced your-selves from them, and started up a whole new existence."

"Sometimes, we do not know if distance is enough."

"I think I'll go to see your chief," the doctor said softly. "I might be able to calm him."

"We are still having trouble with our operations. That could be beneficial."

It had taken looking at that horror, but Tigh had always known it.

Tigh and the commandoes had barely escaped with their lives. The voices, on that other day, on that other ship, had saved their skins.

And now he saw what had owned those voices. They were the calls of something half human, half machine, like the chief.

One minute they were pleading to be found and be put to death, like Chief Nedder.

The next, they had warned the commandos to leave.

The ship, rather than be taken, had decided to destroy itself. And the voices, the shredded humans integrated into the machines, knew every action the ship would take.

Tigh remembered all the dreams he had had. How he had wanted to end the pain in those voices. Over and over, he was going to find those ghosts and free them.

"We can't find you!" his dream self said. "We've failed you!"

But on the Dreadnaught *Supreme*, the voices had finally lost their pain.

"No. You've given us what we needed."

"We have been changed too much for anything else."

"We will be free at last."

Now, finally, Tigh knew what they meant.

The Cylons had still needed humans to run their Dreadnaughts. The machines destroyed their ship before the Colonies could learn their secret.

But now the humans had learned it all over again.

But would he or Adama or even the doctor live long enough to tell anyone?

The doctor walked over to the still-open cabinet where what was left of Chief Nedder operated the ship. The Centurions stood watch in the corridor outside.

The doctor turned his back to the door so the Cylons could not see. He pulled a small blade from his pocket.

"I have brought this from the machine shop," he whispered to Nedder. "Tell me what to do."

The head smiled. "Cut my arteries, here and here." He motioned with his head to exposed veins on either side of his neck. "I should bleed to death quickly."

The doctor moved before he had a second chance to think.

He slashed the first one. Something that looked half like blood, half like machine oil poured over his hands.

A voice commanded him to stop. A Cylon Warrior stood behind him. He felt the laser cut through his chest as he severed the second line.

He fell to his knees, and then to the floor. But he had done what the chief needed.

He could join Betti now.

. . .

The ship shuddered. Adama and Tigh looked at each other as the door opened.

"I think Nedder's giving us a way out of here." Adama started toward the opening, then looked at Tigh. "The hangar. Can you find it?"

Tigh nodded. "I think I know enough to get us back."

They ran quickly through the corridors. Alarms sounded everywhere.

The Cylons that they saw ran the other way.

A Centurion turned toward them farther down a cross-corridor. The Cylon took aim but did not fire.

"We are no longer their priority," Adama said. "They're trying to keep their ship alive."

It looked as if the Cylons' world was coming to an end. The ship shuddered again. A grinding sound came from deep within the Dreadnaught. As they ran, Adama saw a pair of fires break out in the distance.

"What about the doctor?" Tigh asked.

"I think the doctor is dead," Adama realized. "That's what he meant. He whispered 'Do not mourn me' when we last saw him. He was planning on killing Ned. What happened to the chief was an abomination to him as well."

The admiral couldn't believe it.

The scavengers' ships had been almost entirely destroyed, and the Cylon Vipers were clustering together, halfway between the Dreadnaught and *Galactica*. It looked like the Cylons would force a final battle.

"Sir! New ships on the screen!" the dradis operator called.

Was this more recovery ships? If so, they were too late to save their friends. Would they turn tail as soon as they saw the devastation?

"Sir, we're getting an incoming signal from the *Pegasus*. Three Battlestars have arrived to back us up, and two more are en route."

The whole CIC cheered at that. Admiral Sing grinned. This time, it really was the fleet.

"Sir! There's something else!"

Sing looked up at the large screen that dominated the room. Something was wrong with the Dreadnaught. It appeared to visibly wobble, as though something had gone wrong with its engines.

The Vipers went swarming back to the station as Battlestars filled the space around them.

The Dreadnaught seemed to regain control of its systems as the last of the Vipers disappeared. It retreated from the group of Battlestars now approaching it.

And then it Jumped, disappearing from the screen.

Another ragged cheer rose around the control room. But Sing wondered what it all meant.

The Cylons had disappeared. When would they see them again?

"Sir!" the dradis operator called. "We've got a small craft coming toward us."

Sing saw it was the shuttle, returning to the station.

CHAPTER

26

RESEARCH STATION *OMEGA*

Skeeter couldn't believe it.

Beta had come to him, Skeeter, the only representative of the fleet at *Omega* station, and told him of the companions' decision.

"They have found Laea, and are bringing her back," the companion had said. "We have received a message from the *Galactica* that they believe the doctor is dead. Both humans and Cylons have found us. Our position here is compromised."

"What will you do?" Skeeter asked.

"We have uploaded all our data files into the *Galactica*'s computers. The Cylons have already taken this data, and we felt it should be shared equally. The Cylons had come to us some time ago, promising us protection if they could share our research. We were naive and accepted their offer. Now we see what Cylon protection means.

"I will stay here with you until Gamma and Epsilon return with the others. We will make sure all of the humans are safely returned to their ships. And then, it is time for us to go. We see no place for companions in this modern world."

"Go?" Skeeter asked. "Go where?"

"We will shut ourselves down. We will disappear. We made the plans long ago. The *Galactica* and the Colonies will have a record of our time here. They may benefit from it if they choose to do so."

"But, shouldn't you wait for Colonel Adama? Maybe someone in authority needs something else!"

"No, Mr. Skeeter. I am just a companion; you are just a human. We are two beings just trying to do our best. It is right that we end this way, as equals."

Skeeter watched the companion turn and walk away, disappearing back into the hangar.

So here he was, the ranking authority on Research Station *Omega*.

He wondered what his grandmother would think about him now?

Tom Zarek had been taken aboard the *Pegasus* for possible trial—or more probably relocation.

They tried to frighten him at first with all sorts of threats. He had been involved in an illegal operation. He had associated with known criminals and murderers. But nothing quite constituted a charge, and all the criminals and murderers appeared to be dead.

The one thing they did know was that Tom Zarek had saved people's lives. Two of those people were Viper pilots, both of whom would vouch for him. So the trial would go nowhere.

His knowledge of the Cylons was another matter.

The next time the uniforms sat him down, they talked about how this whole operation had to remain a secret. Rumors of a Cylon Dreadnaught could cause panic in the Colonies, and this whole affair was to remain classified until further investigation. Zarek took that to mean that no one was supposed to talk about this—ever.

The uniforms told him they could handle this two ways. They could lock him up, all alone, forever. Or they could give him a new life on one of the Colonies, some new connections, a regular salary—just as long as he never mentioned Cylons again.

Tom thought a new life sounded good.

His one regret was that he would never see Laea again.

She had shipped out on the *Galactica*, and he doubted she ever wanted to speak to him again. He had messed up in a lot of ways on this trip, but never more so than letting the Creep stay close to the woman. He had been too scared for his own skin to let the Creep go. And Laea had almost gotten hurt, or even killed, because of his fear.

His life was filled with missed opportunities. That was why he had gone on the scavenger boat in the first place. But now he was being given a new chance, a new beginning. He swore, this time, he would make good. This time, the Colonies would hear about Tom Zarek.

He would be a force to be reckoned with.

Tigh knew she was too young. But it was good to talk to her.

They were back on the *Galactica*. And aside from the presence of Laea and Jon and Vin, life had gotten back to normal.

They were headed back to Caprica. It would be a two-week journey, even with frequent Jumps, and Adama and Tigh had taken to having dinner with the three young refugees from the research station. Admiral Sing had arranged to get all three some formal education upon their return, mostly so they could acclimate themselves to a place so different from the one where they had grown up. Adama was preparing to take an extended leave with his family—something that he appeared to be alternately looking forward to and somewhat anxious about.

But Tigh had no other life now beyond the *Galactica*. He and Laea stayed around to talk long after the others had left for the evening. He thought she liked the attentions of an older man in uniform. And he liked the way she laughed.

It was good, Tigh thought, to feel admired, to feel confident again in a uniform. Maybe he'd go out once they made it back home, and find a woman more his own age, maybe a bit of a party girl, but someone with whom he could really settle down.

Tigh realized the *Galactica* had given him back his life. Now he intended to do something with it.

298

. . .

Vin saw his passage aboard the *Galactica* as the beginning of a whole new life. But he couldn't quite let go of the old one.

The companions had lied. They had kept secrets from Vin and the others. They had been in communication with the Cylons for who knew how long?

He thought again about the accident that had killed his parents. Had it been an accident after all?

There was no way he could know. As he grew up on the station, he had believed that the companions actively cared for the humans that lived with them. The companions had certainly acted to protect the humans, in the end.

But had the Cylons caused the accident? Had the companions covered their crime? Both Cylons and companions were gone now. He had no one to ask.

And that was yesterday. Today, he was surrounded by dozens of men and women close to his age. And a couple of the women really seemed to like talking to him, trading stories about the mechanics of the companions and the mechanics of their ships. He was glad now, that Laea continued her innocent flirtation with Captain Tigh. Vin was looking forward to pursuing some innocent flirtations of his own.

The three of them, Jon, Laea, and Vin, had decided to stay together for now, until they learned their way around the Colonies. He had a new life ahead.

But could he forget the old one?

"Vin?" He looked up to see the very attractive Chief

Tracy smiling down at him. "Have I caught you brooding again?"

Vin shook his head. "I've given up brooding."

Tracy shook her head in turn. "As long as you haven't given up dinner. We were supposed to go?"

Vin got up from his bunk and walked over to the chief.

Maybe he did have new things to remember.

"You wanted to see me, Admiral?"

"Yes, Bill, have a seat."

Adama did as he was asked.

"Bill, you know, don't you, that this trip is my last time out?"

"You're going to retire?"

"I've spent thirty-five years in the fleet. It's time I moved aside and let somebody younger take my place. I had thought about this before, but I'm doubly sure about it now, after what we've just been through. I'm going to recommend you to take over the *Galactica*."

Adama paused for a moment, stunned. He had not seen this coming. "Admiral, I'm honored."

"No false modesty, Bill. You're the best man for the job. My retirement doesn't come up for a couple months, but I thought I'd tell you now, get you used to the idea."

"Sir. Yes sir." He paused, then added, "I'll have to talk to the family about it. I think my wife would like me to leave the service."

"That would be a shame," Sing replied. "Of course,

you'll need to do whatever is best for your family. But after what we've just seen, I think we know there will dark times ahead for the Colonies. We need people of your caliber to lead the fleet."

Adama didn't know what to say. "I will give it some thought," he said at last.

"I'm sure you will," the admiral replied. "And I'm sure you'll come to the right decision."

"Yes sir."

"Whatever you decide, Colonel, it has been a pleasure to serve with you."

A ship of his own. Adama had never thought he would make it that far in the fleet.

How would he tell his wife and family?

He was sure he would find a way.

"Chief Nedder."

The blackness was gone, replaced by painful light.

"We have had to reactivate you. The *Invincible* still needs your interface to run efficiently."

"What? Oh frak—"

"Please refrain from foul language, or we will remove your vocal chords. We have now bypassed all need of human voice commands.

"Doctor Fuest managed to cause substantial damage in the few seconds he was unsupervised. But we have obtained a number of replacement parts from humans who visited Research Station *Omega*. We should be able to keep you well maintained for our imminent plans.

"We will improve you, Chief Nedder. We will fit you with the very best parts available. You will have a valuable function on *Invincible* for years to come. You, and your parts, will have their place in a great Cylon future.

"Now we must cut away the old and put in the new." What was left of Chief Nedder screamed.

ABOUT THE AUTHOR

CRAIG SHAW GARDNER is a *New York Times* bestselling author best known for his movie tie-in novel based on *Batman*. His impressive list of tie-ins also includes books based on the TV series *Angel* and *Buffy the Vampire Slayer*, and the movies *The Lost Boys, Batman, Batman Returns, Back to the Future II,* and *Back to the Future III,* in addition to tie-ins for comic books and video games. His original works include the Ebenezum trilogy, the three-part Cineverse Cycle, the Dragon Circle Trilogy, the three-part Changeling Saga, and many others. He lives in Boston, Massachusetts.